FRIGHTFUL FOLKLORE
OF
NORTH AMERICA

WATKINS
Sharing Wisdom
Since 1893

FRIGHTFUL FOLKLORE

OF
NORTH AMERICA

ILLUSTRATED FOLK HORROR FROM GREENLAND TO THE PANAMA CANAL

WRITTEN AND ILLUSTRATED BY MIKE BASS

FRIGHTFUL FOLKLORE OF NORTH AMERICA
By Mike Bass

First published in the UK and USA in 2024 by Watkins, an imprint of Watkins Media Limited, Unit 11, Shepperton House, 83–93 Shepperton Road, London N1 3DF

enquiries@watkinspublishing.com

Publisher: Fiona Robertson
Managing Editor: Daniel Culver
Head of Design: Karen Smith
Copyediting: Kate Crossland-Page
Proofreading: JCS Publishing Services Ltd.
Indexing: Lisa Footit
Production: Uzma Taj

Commissioned Artwork and Design Concept: Mike Bass

A CIP record for this book is available from the British Library

ISBN: 978-1-78678-872-6 (Hardback)
ISBN: 978-1-78678-911-2 (eBook)

10 9 8 7 6 5 4 3 2
Printed in Bosnia and Herzegovina
Colour reproduction by by Rival Colour UK

www.watkinspublishing.com

DEDICATION

To Natalie, color consultant, endless listener to all my mad ramblings, collaborator on all things, believer of all my ghost stories, road trip companion, my wife and best friend. You make my world so much less frightening.

·····❧ CONTENTS ☙·····

⁓ FOREWORD ⁓
BY V. CASTRO

Humans have always told stories. Cave drawings by our earliest ancestors record their tales in the only way they knew how. Storytelling, or more specifically folklore, serves as entertainment, explanation of the unknown, a time capsule, and connection. As a storyteller of Mexican heritage, folklore takes me back in in time to my own ancestors. What did they want to say to future generations about the world they lived in? What hidden seeds of knowledge did they feel important to preserve? Why tell stories that are terrifying? Some of their experiences were truly frightening, but terror has a way of rooting into our memories. Folk horror can transport us to places we don't dare to venture. And that is part of the lure, of what makes it even scarier. We don't know who first told the tale, but we do know it exists and it must come from somewhere. There is a chance it could be true. A tree may not always be just a tree and what you consider the sound of wind at dusk could be much more.

The Mexican tale of La Llorona is one of these horrific stories. A woman murders her children then commits suicide. I've drawn on this tale in *The Haunting of Alejandra* (2023) to speak about trauma, mental health, and post-natal depression, something surely the ancestors encountered, but did not have a medical definition for. Jayro Bustamante used the tale in the film *La Llorona* (2019) to speak about the real genocide of the Indigenous population in Guatemala in 1982. Because of the murky beginnings of a folktale, it can fluidly express both new and old horrors.

In the book *Piñata* (2023) by Leopoldo Gout, the ancient horror is unearthed in an excavation. But as the tale unwinds, you learn about the true horror and origins of a party favorite – a piñata. Just because a civilization no longer remains or beliefs in deities have given way to a dominant religion or science, doesn't erase the impact they have on the tales that are told about them. Or on the people who hear their stories.

Warnings can be drawn from the dark recesses of folklore. The horror that lurks in the deepest part of a lake or forest could have kept youngsters safe, stopped them wandering too far from the village. Today our lives are filled with different types of chaos, not usually caused by wild animals or the destructive power of the elements. However, the fundamental emotions and fears are the same. Our inner lives and imaginations have not evolved in the same way our surroundings have. We still feel very tied to folktales and the magic or horror they stir within. It's a primal, deep feeling. I don't think we will ever escape the need to look to the past to explain or understand our present conditions. And as we see in books like *Never Whistle at Night* (2023), an anthology of Indigenous horror, the themes in tales told by people long ago still dwell within us. They shapeshift to fit into the context of our modern world.

The brilliance of *Frightful Folklore of North America* is how it captures the expansiveness of the land, the various cultures (Native and non-Native), the stories told over time. People from all corners of the world have found themselves in this grand space called North America. You see how the rugged terrain and the weather itself sparked fear in the inhabitants and those who found themselves settling here. What could be more frightful than an unknown wilderness or a new people? We move to more modern times, and see how the fears evolve. The tales range from creatures lurking in the frigid waters of Canada, to a hotel haunted by a doomed lover during the Gold Rush, to the beloved and well-known yeti and sasquatch, to a young bride in the colonies executed for murder without proof, all the way down to the Caribbean islands where monsters stalk the night. This impressive collection will haunt your imagination in the best of ways.

I hope you enjoy these wonderful tales as much as I did and perhaps find yourself retelling them so they may live on.

V. CASTRO IS THE TWICE BRAM STOKER-NOMINATED AUTHOR OF TERRIFYING BOOKS INCLUDING *GODDESS OF FILTH* (2021), *THE HAUNTING OF ALEJANDRA* (2023) AND *IMMORTAL PLEASURES* (2024). SHE HAS BEEN WRITING HORROR STORIES SINCE SHE WAS A CHILD, ALWAYS FASCINATED BY MEXICAN FOLKLORE AND THE URBAN LEGENDS OF TEXAS.

·····❦❧ INTRODUCTION ❦❧·····

Shadows scurry through the wood, hidden within the underbrush. In the darkness lurks something darker still, barely visible yet definitely there.

It's here, at the edge of the small circle of civilization provided by the light of the campfire, that fear claims dominion. Our pulse quickens, sending our hearts pounding. The crack of a branch sets our thoughts racing; a gust of wind calls every hair on our body to stand at attention. It's here, just beyond the warm glow of the flames, that the tales in this book originate.

Culture upon culture, civilization after civilization, from the Indigenous peoples to all those who have settled North America over the past half millennium: each one has added their stories to this ghastly anthology. Some of these horribly grim tales were almost lost to the passing of time, but they refused to fall completely from our consciousness and now are being given new life in these pages. Other tales are well known, they have frightened us around campfires and in the eerie glow of flashlights held below chins for years.

These frightfully dismal tales are the original folk horror, the lifeblood of contemporary horror. At the cinema we watch movies such as *The Wendigo* (2022) and *Antlers* (2021), which draw on Indigenous Tales of a ravenous and never-sated monster. Many of the scary movies we love, from *The Blair Witch Project* (1999) to *The Curse of La Llorona* (2019) and *Hereditary* (2018), are built on psychological fear, on an unseen yet ever-present threat to us and our loved ones. As in folklore, we see the protagonists deal with subjects that are taboo, and have to weigh their decisions against social norms and deal with entities which, although intangible, must be avoided at all costs.

Collected from old tomes or unearthed in the dark recesses of online libraries, heard from the mouths of our elders, passed from one generation to another, these tales are not for the faint of heart. Be warned: once read, these stories will linger in your thoughts, especially in those moments just before you switch of the light for a fitful night's unrest.

Still, many of us actively seek out the very things that scare us most. For us it's the rush we feel from a frightening experience, the physical and mental reaction our bodies have to fear. Physically, fear sends a small organ located

in the middle of our brain, the amygdala, into overdrive, alerting our nervous system in the process. Flooding our bodies with adrenaline and cortisol, our heart rate quickens, raising our blood pressure and altering the very flow of our blood. Our breathing gets faster and shallower and our arteries dilate in order to carry more oxygen-saturated blood to our extremities, preparing arms to swing in defense and legs to carry us away to safety. As with the bravery bestowed by a stiff drink, even our inhibitions and ability to make sound judgments are impaired, as the amygdala pulls function from the cerebral cortex, the part of the brain that controls reasoning. Our reactions to fear are instinctual, even primal. That boost of energy which heightened our senses and made us stronger and faster is what helped keep our prehistoric ancestors stay alive.

Yet, when we're in a safe environment such as the comfort of our home, watching a movie, listening to a podcast or reading a book, this ancient physical response to fear provides quite a thrill. And the exact moment of terror is not even the only joy we get from the experience. Our mind and body remain in a heightened state of arousal long after the frightening moment is over, as our body emits pleasure-enducing dopamine for hours afterward.

The key to our enjoyment of horror is the knowledge that we're safe from it. That when something becomes too unsettling, too scary or too much for us to handle, we can remove ourselves from it. Ultimately, we know that we have control of the situation; by simply closing a book or turning off a movie or podcast, we can take away the cause of our fear. This control provides comfort through security, and the knowledge of this security allows us to safely experience situations that would be unbearable in our real lives, to venture into dangerous places. Horror lets us travel through the shadowed aspects of the human experience, to explore the transgressive and satisfy our curiosity as we peek through the cracks in our minds into the darkest parts of our imagination. Through horror we can spend time away from the reality of our own lives. Horror offers an opportunity to briefly escape our responsibilities, to push aside our jobs, our sadnesses, our worries and our concerns about what's happening in the wider world as we grapple with this story being laid out before us. Horror gives us an outlet for stress – providing, through perceptions of threat and feelings of fear and dread, a sort of pressure release for the pent-up anxiety our bodies hold on to, helping us to be more psychologically resilient.

HORROR COMES TO NORTH AMERICA

It isn't well understood how the first humans made their way to North America. The ice ages would have made migration by foot nearly impossible, and the oceans have always offered a formidable barrier. Somehow, they found a way, and with them they brought all their hopes, desires and, of course, fears.

Crossing into this new world of vast fields of ice and immense thick forests, these early humans would have had to discover how to survive in an unfamiliar land that was flush with other living beings. Some would have been familiar to them, including prey such as mastodons, deer and moose, as well as animals that would have posed a threat to them, such as bears, wolves and the big cats. But they also would have encountered the unfamiliar; creatures unlike anything they had ever seen before. Surely these encounters laid the foundation for the stories and folklore passed down through generation after generation in these new lands in which they were struggling for their existence. Perhaps this is when tales such as those about the fearsome and hairy wild men, the Sasquatch (page 79), or the diminutive, gnome-like, needle-toothed Mîmîkwîsiwak (page 64) were first shared.

Over the next 26,000 years, humans spread across this large continent in all directions. New habitats resulted in new challenges, forcing the early inhabitants of North America to evolve, and so too did their fears. Each group of people formed different traditions and belief systems, in which old spirits and fears melded with the new attitudes and ideas that grew from the unique experiences in their new homes.

The Indigenous peoples of North America understood that if their relationships with the land and the animals that lived on it were unbalanced, this could bring humans great misfortune and even death. In the frozen lands of the north, the original inhabitants suffered stark winters and faced starvation. In the arid south, the sun was all-powerful and people feared the absence of rain. Tales of fear, such as those of the child-snatching Qallupilluit who dwelled below the ice (page 24), the ravenous and cannibalistic wendigo (page 90) of the Great Lakes regions of the United States and Canada, and the shy, reclusive and fiercely territorial Ste-ye-hah'-mah of the Pacific northwest, who hunted humans covered in sticks and mud as if the forest itself had come to life (page 33), speak of people's struggle to survive in harsh environments.

It was only a matter of time before the exploration of the seas led to the arrival of Europeans in North America. It's believed that the Norse were the first to traverse the northern Atlantic, hopping from island to island until eventually making their way to the frozen shores of Greenland and northeastern Canada by mid-900 CE. Some 500 years later, Spain and England found their way across the Atlantic: Spain to the tropical shores of the Caribbean and Central America, and England to the frigid north of the Canadian coast. They were soon followed by France and the Netherlands. The nations of Europe claimed new territories and their rich resources, squabbling over who had the right to exploit them first.

Over the next three centuries, the empires of Europe raced to establish colonies in this newly "discovered" land, laying claim to territory that was not theirs for the taking. And crossing the Atlantic along with the troops, setttler and supplies in the vessels of the colonists came their traditions, religion, superstitions and fears. Belief in spirits and witches, in the fae folk and little people, as well as the fear of Satan and his host of demons, and of the Almighty Himself. Some of these beliefs fuelled the atrocities against the Indigenous peoples of North America that the colonizers were to enact there.

For those the Indigenous peoples who already called this continent home, a terror unlike anything they had ever known before entered their lives. Disease, forced migration, land seizure and the death of millions. For the Black peoples transported here from Africa, this new land meant forced labor, slavery with millions of associated deaths and the subjugation of generations of families. Horror acquired a whole new meaning.

The centuries passed as cultures collided, and war, imported sickness, slavery, exploitation and the harshness of the elements saw millions perish. The traditions of Europe and those of the Indigenous peoples of North America reluctantly bonded, and histories became intertwined. People of all colors came here, from all over the world, bringing their traditions, beliefs and folktales, their taboos, fears and terrors, adding their stories to North America's great body of folklore.

As traditions evolved, so too did fears. Tales of little people, who once might have responded to gifts and kindness with generosity in return, were meaner here and swift to move from playfulness to anger; creatures such as the Chichiricús (page 169) of the Caribbean now sought blood. Spirits who had once offered warnings and insights to the living, here in

the stark and desolate lands of the plains were more vengeful; the Banshee of the Badlands (page 112), for example, who doled out retribution to those who did not answer her cries for mercy, or the phantom who haunts Deadman's Pond (page 37) in a gloomy pool in New Brunswick and now seeks vengeance for the circumstances of his death.

Whether it's because of the way fear has responded to the unholy tragedy that was the creation of North America, or because folklore has been shaped by the harsh conditions and awesome terrain that people faced when they first arrived at some point in the continent's long history – the vast deserts and humid rainforests, the inpenetrable jungle, monstrous mountain ranges and never-ending plains – this folklore is surely among the world's most terrifying.

In these pages you will find just some of the stories of North America. Read on if you dare and discover the frightful folklore spawned by the wilderness, harshness and tragedy of this continent.

FRIGHTFUL
FOLKLORE
OF
NORTH AMERICA

❧ VALLEY OF THE HEADLESS MEN ❧
NORTHWEST TERRITORIES ⁕ CANADA

For more than ten thousand years, the Dene people have lived in the shadows of jagged mountains and the dense forests of the Nahanni Valley, which is also known as the Valley of the Headless Men.

It was the Gold Rush of the late 1800s that brought the first settlers to this wild, remote and inhospitable land. While the masses flocked to the Yukon, in the spring of 1906 two brothers, Willie and Frank McLeod, decided to set out to find gold in the Nahanni Valley. Two years later, their headless remains were discovered.

Ten years after the McLeod brothers had tried to find gold, Martin Jorgensen, who had just sent word home that he had "struck it rich," was also found dead. His cabin had been burned to the ground and his charred remains were found upriver. Just like the McLeods, Jorgensen was missing his head.

Over the next 50 years, the dead bodies continued to pile up in the Nahanni Valley. In 1927, the skeleton of a known outlaw and occasional prospector, Yukon Fisher, was found in the same location as the McLeod brothers' bodies. Fisher still had his head and his death was unexplained. In 1931, the headless corpse of Phil Powers was found in a pile of ash. In 1945, Ernest Savard was discovered headless alongside the charred remains of his tent. That same year, the frozen body of an experienced hunter and trapper named John O'Brien was found next to his extinguished campfire, with a box of matches in one hand and a match that had been fired in the other. It was noted that it looked as though an arctic wind had blown in, extinguished his fire, and frozen his corpse in an instant, but no wind of such power has ever been recorded in reality.

Strange as the stories of these bodies are, the tales of those who have gone missing are just as bizarre. One such story is that of Anne Laferte, who vanished from a hunting party in 1926. She was last seen in the middle of the night by another hunter who had been woken by the sound of vigorous splashing in the river. He claimed that when he looked out, he saw Laferte clambering up the scree on the other side of the river on all fours, completely naked. He recalled that she returned his stare with a wild look on her face. Horrified, he sheepishly retreated into his tent for a restless night. Anne Laferte was never seen again.

In 1929, Angus Hall, a gold prospector, vanished without a trace. In 1936, prospectors William Eppler and Joseph Mulholland also went missing. Their cabin had been burned to the ground, but their bodies were never found.

After May Lafferty wandered off from her hunting party, she was tracked into the woods. Her trail often vanished – sometimes at the edge of cliffs or along the river where rapids would have thwarted a crossing – only to be picked up again further upstream. Trackers found Lafferty's clothing along the trail, one discarded item after another; it seemed she had been wandering the wilds completely naked. The trail eventually went cold, and no one knows what happened to her.

Today, much of the region remains unexplored on foot, although satellite mapping offers us a good look at the area. Some of the valley's features have been named according to the fates of those who lost their lives there: Headless Creek, Deadmen Valley, and the Funeral Range – mountains which cast long shadows across the surrounding land.

An interesting perspective on these stories is offered by the macabre tales shared by the Indigenous Dene people over the centuries. From these we learn that they were repeatedly terrorized by a vicious, cannibalistic tribe called the Naha who lived further north.

When the Dene finally tired of the Naha's attacks, they traveled upriver to put an end to the mischief. When they arrived at the Naha's camp, however, no one was there – it looked as though the Naha people had simply walked off into the wilderness. As the Dene traveled home, the sun slowly sank over the western peaks and darkness crept toward them. The breeze that had cooled them by day suddenly turned into an ice-cold gale. As gusts tore at their shelters and a tempest raged, the Dene people huddled together, back-to-back, scanning the wilderness beyond their fires. What they feared could not be seen – a continuous wailing, combined with a nagging insistence to flee. They heard unearthly shrieks and screams that seemed to rise and fall with the howling wind. In that instant, it felt as though Mother Nature had turned her gaze toward them, and was displeased that they were there.

TO WARD OFF ANY MALICIOUS SPIRITS THAT MAY MEAN THEM HARM
DRIVE AN OLD AND COARSE

IRON NAIL

INTO THE HEAD OF A NEWBORN'S CRIB

NEVER ENTER A CEMETERY WITHOUT A HAT

LEST A SPIRIT HOP ON YOUR BACK AND RIDE
UPON YOU OUT THROUGH THE COLD IRON GATE

MIND YOU HOLD YOUR BREATH!

AS THE SPIRITS ARE KEEN TO ENTER YOUR BODY UPON YOUR BREATH

BEWARE

THE SQUEAKY HINGE OF A DOOR!

TROUBLESOME SPIRITS AND THE DOWNTRODDEN SOULS
WHO ENDLESSLY WANDER MAY FIND THE CREAKS AND GROANS AS
AN INVITATION TO MAKE A HOME OF THEIR OWN IN YOUR HOUSE

KEEP AN OIL CAN AT THE READY!

GOOD LUCK AND FORTUNE COMES WHEN ONE IS WELCOMED BY

A STRAY BLACK CAT!

DOOM AND CALAMITY IF ONE APPROACHES AND TURNS AWAY
BEFORE MAKING YOUR ACQUAINTANCE

❧❦ QALLUPILLUIT ❦❧

NUNAVUT * CANADA

In the far north of the Arctic, the different seasons bring constant change to the sea ice. As the frigid air gets warmer in the spring, the ice thins, and large thaw holes open up, causing violent downrushes of meltwater. As the warmth of fall gradually wanes, the ocean begins its annual freeze, and the surface of the water ices over, giving the deceptive appearance of solid, traversable land. This is the ever-changing environment in which the Qallupilluit stalk their prey – young children foolhardy and brazen enough to play at the edges of the icy sea.

Making a home in the frozen arctic waters, the Qallupilluit spend most of their time in pursuit of small children to steal. Swimming below the ice, they look for little shadows cast on the surface above. Once they have found their prey, the Qallupilluit try to draw the children ever closer, by knocking and tapping on the ice, by humming a familiar lullaby, or by mimicking the sounds of the children's parents. No matter the means, the end is always the Qallupilluits' sole pursuit – the snatching of children.

None of the children that the Qallupilluit have stolen have ever returned, and no one knows why they are taken. Those who are hopeful believe that the Qallupilluit are lonely and want a bit of company in their underwater lairs, while others believe the children are put to work, ceaselessly toiling, catering to a Qallupilluk's every want and need. But those who know the true nature of this desolate and unforgiving land presume that all the Qallupilluits' cunning and endless hunting is simply to satisfy their insatiable hunger for human flesh.

Inuit elders say that when the ocean becomes uneasy, or when a cold fog rises from the surface, a Qallupilluk – with her scaly green skin, long black hair and keen-edged, black and jagged claws – is lurking in angry waters just below the ice, waiting, patient and wanting, ravenous and hungry.

Once she has small ones in her grasp, they will never be seen again. Any hope of finding them will come to nought, but this doesn't mean the torment is over. The Qallupilluit often mercilessly mock the parents of stolen children, crying out in the voices of their lost ones for days after they've gone missing, haunting those left behind.

BE WARY OF THE
AURORA BOREALIS

THESE ARE THE SPIRITS OF THE DEAD LEADING LOST SOULS TO A BETTER PLACE
TAKE CARE TO NOT DRAW THEIR ATTENTION TO YOURSELF
CARRY A KNIFE AS PROTECTION WHEN THE LIGHTS ARE AT THEIR BRIGHTEST

THE FORTUITOUSNESS OF A FOX BEFORE YOU

**TO SEE A FOX CROSS THE PATH AHEAD OF YOU
YOUR TRAVELS WILL BE SWIFT AND UNDIFFICULT**

THE MISFORTUNE OF A FOX BEHIND YOU

**TO SEE A FOX CROSS THE PATH BEHIND YOU
YOUR TRAVELS WILL BE SLOW AND BURDENSOME**

**NEVER OFFEND THE CREATURES OF THE SEA WITH
THE PRESENCE OF AN ANIMAL OF THE LAND**

CLEANSE YOUR WEAPONS BEFORE YOU HUNT ON LAND AFTER YOU'VE HUNTED THE SEA
NEVER CONSUME THE WALRUS ON THE SAME DAY AS THE CARIBOU
NOR WEAR THE HIDES OF A BEAR TO HUNT FOR A SEAL

DO NOT WHISTLE AT NIGHT

IT ATTRACTS THE BAD SPIRITS OF THE WOOD

NEVER WEAR YOUR SHOES
ON THE WRONG FEET!

YOU RISK COMING FACE TO FACE WITH A BEAR IN THE WILD!

DO NOT PLAY GAMES AT A FUNERAL • IT ATTRACTS THE SPIRITS OF THE DEAD TO JOIN IN
THEY DON'T ALWAYS FOLLOW THE SAME RULES AS THE LIVING!

⋯꧁ SCARY MARY ꧂⋯
ALASKA * UNITED STATES

Dwight had a dream of making his fortune in gold, and Mary, who loved him dearly, decided to tag along for the ride. In the early spring of 1898, they boarded a ship and set sail to the burgeoning city of Skagway, Alaska.

According to their plan, Mary would stay in Skagway while Dwight went to the gold fields, and they'd marry when he returned that fall as a rich man. Having paid six months' rent upfront for Room 23 at the Golden North Hotel, Mary comfortably settled in, and Dwight eagerly set out on foot to make his fortune.

Like many fast-growing cities of the American frontier, Skagway was a cobbled together, amalgamated mess of a city. There were more taverns, brothels, opium dens and gambling halls than there were general stores and churches, and more criminals, barmen and prostitutes than lawful citizens. Mary knew it was in her best interests to spend most of her time in her room, and for four months she did just that – awaiting Dwight's return, looking out of the window for hours, hoping to catch the first glimpse of him striding down the road with a fortune in his bags.

Unfortunately, that day never came. The unforgiving nature of the Klondike, where damp and cold permeated every nook and cranny, meant the place was rife with illness. Mary contracted pneumonia and died after crawling to the window wearing the dress she was meant to wear for her wedding once Dwight returned.

The cruelty of Skagway knew no limits, and only days after Mary had passed away, Dwight returned to the city after striking it rich. As it turned out, he had not only found gold in the Yukon – he'd also married another woman. Dwight and his new bride swiftly set sail back to Seattle.

Mary's spirit remained in Skagway, and for years afterwards, guests and employees of the hotel reported seeing a woman gazing out of the window of Room 23 and hearing forlorn wails throughout the night. As the decades went on, Mary became restless, angry and resentful. Doors would slam and a spectral woman would race down the halls. The lucky guests in Room 23 experienced loud knocks and inexplicable blasts of frigid air. The unlucky guests woke in the middle of the night choking on their breath, feeling overcome with the sensation of heartbreaking loss.

··❦ TUPILAK ❦··
GREENLAND

After five years under the frozen ground, the child's body has minimal decay, but its desiccated skin is stretched tightly across its cheekbone and brow. A shallow resemblance of its living self, this shriveled, nameless child will soon serve a greater purpose.

The wronged woman cuts off the corpse's head and carefully stitches its leathery skin to the upper torso of a large dog. She removes the dog's paws and replaces them with the talons of an eagle. She takes out the child's teeth and inserts shards of jagged whale bone in their vacant cavities, creating a shark's grimace. The hindquarters of an elk, recently perished but already ravished by scavengers, become the legs.

She places her creation near a water source and, kneeling down beside it, she thrusts a small bundle – a lock of hair wrapped in a piece of cotton, tied with a bit of fish intestine – into its chest cavity. While speaking words intently over the body, she blankets it in fresh veridian moss and bilberry leaves, then departs.

A few days later, the creature awakens and chokes out its first breath. As it cries out in hunger, the woman lays in the moss beside it, cradles its withered head in her arms and feeds it from her own breast. For three long weeks she cares for it in her home, watching it grow stronger, larger and more dangerous. Soon, the creature no longer craves breast milk, and instead eats the rodents that scurry about the small cabin. The time has come to set it out on its task. She leads it back to the riverside, kneels down in the damp moss, and whispers a name, a place, and a vengeful deed – long overdue – in the creature's ear. It stands with determination, its dead eyes focused on the horizon, its jaw gritted, its taloned fists clenched. For just a moment it pauses before it departs into the night.

The woman returned home contented. But several weeks later, while she was pondering the progress of her tupilak, wondering whether those who had wronged her had now been vanquished, there came a thunderous crash at the door. There, on her threshold, stood her creation, her spell undone, his purpose reversed. It was a risk she had knowingly taken. Before she could say a word, or even hold up a hand in protest, the tupilak was upon her, tearing into her, pulling her to pieces bit by bit. This creature of her own making, revenge made flesh and bone, had found its way home.

⸺ STE-YE-HAH'-MAH ⸺
PACIFIC NORTHWEST

Long ago, they were like any other tribe – a reclusive people who lived on the edges of the wilderness. Wary of outsiders, they were not what you'd call kind, but they weren't malicious either. They simply kept to their own, and left others to theirs.

As time passed – a hundred generations or more – they became more reclusive. Once a lean and strong people, years of solitude and hiding means they are now bent, wiry and gaunt – wild and rough creatures who no longer see themselves as human, but instead as hunters of humans. Their once lusciously thick black hair now hangs lank over their emotionless, angular and hollow-eyed faces. Even their speech is no longer human, and they instead communicate via the pops and clicks of snapping twigs, the sighs and groans of bending trees, and the songs of birds and cries of animals.

Many call them the invisible tribe, because you will not see them, even if they are near. You will know they are there, however, when an inscrutable eeriness raises the hairs on the back of your neck, when the sound of the wood is not quite as it should be, or when there is an unfamiliar scent on the air. And when you fall into disorientation, then a state of high anxiety.

When the tribe come for you, covered in soil and clay and dressed in twigs and sticks, it seems as though the forest itself has come to life – brush and bramble begin to stalk you. Many who are caught are carried back to a hidden camp, and are then strung up and clumsily butchered. If they are hungry, they may tear their prey to shreds on the spot in a ravenous blood feast. If stolen children are young enough, they are kept and raised as the tribe's own, and taken women are often kept as wives. Regardless of what becomes of those who fall into their hands, one truth remains constant – they will never be seen again.

The tribe turn to wildness has evolved into an aggressive rapaciousness, and they strike with brutal and immediate cruelty against anyone they view as being disrespectful to them or their land, regardless of the victim's intention. Just saying the tribe's name out loud, Ste-ye-hah'-mah, can be provocation enough. The best form of defense, therefore, is to never speak of them at all.

⋯⋰⋰ ERLAVEERSINIOOQ ⋱⋱⋯
GREENLAND

The horizon blended into the sunless sky as a winter gale raged. Gusts of wind blew wave after wave of snow in all directions. For the two men to continue would be folly, but to stop would mean freezing to death.

By nightfall, the storm had finally passed, and as the moon rose, full and brilliant, at last the men had an opportunity to check their bearings. The stars seemed off, a bit too western, a little too low in the sky, but westward the pair were headed, so westward they would continue. In time, they came upon a small, dimly lit cabin. Smoke rising from the chimney meant there was a fire, warmth and perhaps the kind offer of a good meal inside.

They knocked on the door, and in a short time it swung open to reveal a large woman, scantily dressed with only a piece of hide swung loosely around her waist. Her breasts hung heavily down to her navel, and her belly was full and round. Standing shamelessly at the door, her head was wide – somehow, impossibly, it was wider than it was tall – her nose merely two broad nostrils, large black holes below her massive, wide-set eyes. She looked the men up and down as if sizing them up. The corners of her full lips turned up slightly as she pulled her lower lip in, then slowly released it while her broad tongue wetted her upper lip to reveal a broad, gap-toothed smile. She invited them in and offered them a seat at her table.

She turned to the fire and ladled out two generous helpings of stew from a big pot. As she turned, parts of her body swung about and clapped against other parts. Two dead sculpin fish dangled down between her heavy thighs, swinging back and forth as she crossed the room. Her large eyes and broad smile flashed as she placed their meals before them. The absurdity of it all finally proved to be too much, and one of the men burst into laughter.

Immediately, her smile came undone, revealing angry gnashing teeth. She leapt over the table and slashed the laughing man open at his belly with a knife. Standing astride him, she began to gather up his innards, his liver, kidneys, lungs and heart.

The second man stood in frozen astonishment as she gave a hearty whistle, and the pot where the stew had been cooking scurried across the room to act as a repository into which the laughing man's organs were casually tossed – her kindness repaid in meat and blood if not repaid in kind.

THE SPIRITS OF DEADMAN'S POND

It isn't completely understood why some bodies of water hold onto their dead, clinging to the spirits of those who have drowned in their depths. Some believe it's because water has the ability to hold on to and conduct energy; to act as a conduit that helps spirits to manifest.

The murky black waters of Deadman's Pond in the Newfoundland town of St John's have long been thought to be bottomless. Some say that deep below its surface there are caverns and tunnels that lead out to the sea. It sits in the shadow of Gibbet's Hill, where public executions were carried out during the early years of colonization. For convicted pirates and criminals, death came at the end of a rope and their corpses were then hung high on the hill in metal gibbets, to serve as a gruesome reminder to stay on the right side of the law.

Once the bodies had decayed, their bones picked clean by crows and flies, what little of them remained was then placed in a barrel weighted down with rocks, and was rolled into the pond, sending their souls, so it was thought, directly to hell. But if the hauntings are any indication, not all of those souls remained in the underworld.

For years, tales of spirits sinfully lurking in Deadman's Pond have endured. Its deep waters lie placid on calm days, masking the malicious scheming of the spirits who reside just below the surface. Some who have swum there tell of the sensation of small fish darting about their legs, followed by a startling firm grasp around their ankle, and a heavy weight pulling them down. Others have experienced unusual currents pushing them away from shore, away from their family and friends. Some speak of spectral hands reaching up from the darkness of the depths below, or out toward the shore, grabbing for those who find themselves too close to the pond's edge, clutching victims and pulling them beneath the water's surface.

There are many folks looking for reasons behind the number of unexplained drownings at the small pond over the years. The conventionally minded might suggest that it's the pond's chilly waters, or the unexpected depth and rapid drop-offs; that "without explanation" is just another way of saying "careless or foolish behavior." But no amount of rational reasoning will change the minds of those who have experienced firsthand the strange occurrences at Deadman's Pond.

MAHAHA

Laughing boosts the immune system, increases our intake of oxygen, strengthens organ and muscle function, and helps in coping with stress. The endorphins released when we laugh give us an emotional boost and can help to diminish pain. It is often said, therefore, that laughter is the best medicine. But far north in the frozen Arctic, the Mahaha is proof that too much laughter can be a bad thing, and could even be deadly.

At first, you might only notice the strange, carved shapes in the ice and rock – curious formations and structures built of snow. When you hear a faint maniacal giggling in the distance, however, you know that you are being stalked by the Mahaha. At first, he tries to confuse you, causing disagreements and discord among the members of your group, deliberately creating animosity and, eventually, division. When people begin to break off to try to make a go of it alone, this is when the Mahaha strikes.

Barefoot and barely clothed, the Mahaha stands still against the frozen horizon. His eyes – peering at his victims through a tangle of ragged black, filthy and frozen hair – are haunting and blank, pale white and frosted, as emotionless as his twisted rictus grin. Despite his stillness, the unnerving shriek of his incessant giggling, scattered and uneasy, derisive and indecent, is always echoing around you. This situation can continue indefinitely, the Mahaha mocking you both night and day, always finding ways to surprise you, and at each encounter slowly creeping a step or two closer toward you.

With each move, his appearance becomes more visible – ice-blue skin and a withered form, meager and sinewy, as if gnawed away by the frigid arctic winds. But it is the Mahaha's hands that reveal his true and vicious nature – each of his fingers bears a long, sharp and broken claw. When he finally makes his attack, it is with a simple stroke of a finger that the Mahaha induces uncontrollable fits of laughter in his victim. As his prey laughs, unable to regain composure, the Mahaha drains their very life force, consuming their energy, leaving behind an emaciated and frozen husk. Appearing outwardly as if they had frozen to death, the deceased are left with a telltale sign that the Mahaha is to blame for their demise – a twisted, forever-frozen grimace.

SETTLER LORE

IN THE VASTNESS OF THE WILDS

KINDNESS IS HARD TO COME BY

NEVER PASS UP A FREE MEAL NOR COMPLAIN ABOUT THE COOK NOR PRACTICE INGRATITUDE

ALWAYS BE THANKFUL

NEVER RETURN BORROWED SALT · IT ENDS A FRIENDSHIP AND SOWS CONTEMPT

• UNLUCKY 13 •

A MOST UNFORTUNATE NUMBER

THE THIRTEENTH GUEST MUST LEAVE, OR FIND A PARTNER TO EVEN THE NUMBER

THIRTEEN AT A DINNER ENSURES A HIGHLY UNDIGESTABLE MEAL

A THIRTEENTH PENNY MUST BE THROWN AWAY

NEVER BEGIN A JOB ON FRIDAY

THE WORK WILL NEVER PROSPER
YOU WILL NOT LIVE TO SEE IT FINISHED

NOT A SINGLE WOMAN OUT OF A HUNDRED

WOULD WILLINGLY START MAKING A GARMENT

ON A FRIDAY OUT OF FEAR OF NEVER SEEING IT WORN

NEITHER PICK NOR EAT THE BERRIES OF THE MID-OCTOBER BRAMBLE

THEY ARE PAST THEIR TIME
AND SURELY HAVE BEEN CLAIMED BY THE DEVIL HIMSELF

⁂ ISLE OF DEMONS ⁂

NEWFOUNDLAND AND LABRADOR * CANADA

The notoriously treacherous Strait of Belle Isle lies between the Labrador Peninsula and the island of Newfoundland. The ships of early explorers, who were tempted by one of the richest fishing grounds on the planet, had to contend with heavy fog, almost year-round sea ice, and the strong tidal currents that collided with frigid arctic waters. Even in the face of these threats, what sailors through the centuries feared most of all was a small piece of land called the Isle of Demons. Although this island was one of the most beautiful along the coast, it was uninhabited by humans, due to disturbances caused by the evil beings who had made it their home.

Long before the Europeans entered these waters, the Indigenous Beothuk people knew this place was to be avoided. Although it appeared lush and abundant with flora and fauna, no one dared to cross the water to its shores, as they believed it was the home of the sea demon Aich-mud-yim and his minions – bloodthirsty devils, ghosts and monsters.

When the Vikings arrived, they feared nothing. They took to the beautiful sand beaches of the Isle of Demons in a rush of courage, despite the cacophony of cackling devils and wailing ghosts. They found themselves maliciously harassed day and night by unintelligible voices and horrifying visions of evil spirits. The ensuing bouts of madness resulted in the self-inflicted deaths of the entire Viking crew.

Later, French explorers claimed that, as they sailed along the coast, their ships were buffeted by a great storm, and on the winds that battered them, they heard the incomprehensible murmuring voices of a mass of people. They said the noise was as loud as a busy street in Paris.

Over the centuries, maps have depicted the island as being occupied by beasts and giant birds, sea serpents and devils. Around 1800, though, the island began to disappear entirely from newly drawn maps. Through either a change of name or a simple omission, the Isle of Demons simply seemed to cease to exist.

Despite this strange disappearance, even to this day, when the wind gnashes at the Newfoundland coast on a cold winter's night, an odd voice can still be heard, screaming over the gale.

❦❧ DUNDAS ISLAND BLACKFLY ❦❧
BRITISH COLUMBIA ✳ CANADA

Biting insects have plagued mankind since the beginning of human existence. We despise these bugs for their delivery of swollen bites, and their incessant drone that brings restless anxiety and fitful sleep. We swat and slap and crush, attempting to rid ourselves of their annoying presence. With the exception only of the gentle honeybee's sting – whose loss of life we often lament – we curse these creatures' very being.

Yet the pain these insects cause is nothing compared to the destruction caused by the Dundas Island Blackfly. Growing up to six inches in length, these loathsome critters inhabit a small group of islands across Chatham Sound, where the Alaskan coast sneaks its way down to meet British Columbia. The Dundas Island Blackfly's dull leathery skin, black and as hard and thick as a walnut shell, is covered with coarse hairs. Protruding from its back are two sets of large, iridescent wings, translucent and ink stained, endlessly twitching, incessantly scraping and rattling, like metal grates constantly gnashing against each other. Its obsidian eyes bulge with a thousand rounded and reflective facets. Its legs are like bramble vine, covered in spikey short hairs, and this huge fly has dual tarsals on its feet – thick and sharp as a cat's claws – in order to easily dig into its prey's flesh.

Dundas Island Blackflies hunt in swarms so large that they have been mistaken for starling murmurations by sailors passing the island. Relentless, the blackflies follow their prey for miles, buzzing around their target when it is on the move, pestering and biting it when at rest. These grotesque flies are capable of bringing down a large moose; even the mighty grizzly bear avoids their territory. When they bite, their scissor-like mandibles tear into the prey's skin, slashing and sawing, perforating blood vessels and enlarging the wound. Their saliva causes paralysis and is also an anticoagulant, ensuring the prey's blood will not clot. Every drop of blood is drunk before the flesh is consumed, leaving behind a pile of bones.

The Indigenous peoples of the region refer to these creatures as "Sky Devils," or "Flying Demons." They believe they were released when an ancient people tried to rid the earth of everything bad. Having gathered up all evil beings, creatures and things, the whole collection was cast into a great fire on Dundas Island. As the fire raged, acrid smoke filled the air and up rose a thunderous buzzing and a swirling cloud of ravenous flies in a swarm big enough to blot out the sun.

❦ THE BELL ISLAND SWAMP HAG ❧

NEWFOUNDLAND AND LABRADOR * CANADA

The entire marshland reeks of melancholia – a sadness that has been steeped far too long in the solitude of this small island. The stench of rot lingers heavy on the air, while layer upon layer of dead leaves and detritus fail to provide a solid surface underfoot.

It was in this place she breathed her last breath, in an unfortunate circumstance that would have been avoided if she had arrived either a moment earlier or a moment later.

A group of duplicitous soldiers had gathered at Dobbin's Garden to discuss their deceitful intentions with the townsfolk, only to be interrupted by this hapless young woman. Fearing they would be undone by this witness, two of the men dragged her to the marsh and smothered her face down in the mud, hiding her body among the rest of the rot and decay, never to be found.

This was not the end of her story, however, as her restless spirit still roams the marsh. As twilight falls, you can hear the sound of weeping when traveling the road that passes nearby. Grim, yet somehow earnest in its nature, the noise compels you to stop in your tracks and enter the marsh in pursuit of its source. Driven by a sense of urgency, compulsion takes over and despite the perilousness of the undertaking, you must continue until at last you find her.

Dressed in a pure white gown, she appears as young and beautiful as the day she died. Once seen, she turns and begins to make her way toward you, closer and closer, and the smell of moonflower fills the air. Closer still she comes, until in a moment her color begins to fade. Her dress grays and falls to tatters, her skin sags and slumps over her boney frame. A foul smell fills the air – a paralyzing stench of decay that prohibits your retreat – while her gaze holds you in place. Now right in front of you, she falls to her knees, and her worm-ridden hands pull you to the ground beneath her. Her dark and sunken eyes glare intently at you as she crawls onto your chest, wheezing, until finally, with her face inches from yours and her voice ragged and dry, she gasps, "No one came to help me, now no one will help you. Taste what I tasted. Smell what I smelled."

DANS LES YEUX!

BEWARE A DRINK TOASTED WITHOUT EYE CONTACT

POISON • ILL INTENT • LOATHING • COVETOUSNESS

ONE OR ALL MAY BE HIDDEN BEHIND THE AVOIDED INTERACTION

LA MICHE DE PAIN

THE LOAF OF BREAD

NEVER EAT BOTH ENDS OF A LOAF OF BREAD BEFORE THE MIDDLE

MISFORTUNE WILL FALL UPON YOU BEFORE THE ENTIRE LOAF IS CONSUMED

LA MICHE DE PAIN À L'ENVERS

◆ THE UPSIDE-DOWN LOAF ◆

NEVER PLACE BREAD ON THE TABLE TOPSIDE DOWN!

THIS IS HOW BREAD IS LEFT FOR THE EXECUTIONER

ONLY INCONSOLABLE SADNESS WILL FOLLOW

BEWARE

◆ AN OFFER THAT SOUNDS TOO GOOD TO BE TRUE! ◆

YOU MAY BE SHAKING HANDS WITH THE DEVIL HIMSELF!

NEVER ACCEPT A KNIFE AS A GIFT

IT WILL CUT THE TIES THAT BIND YOU IN FRIENDSHIP

ALWAYS GIVE A COIN IN EXCHANGE • EVEN IF IT IS AN INVALUABLE ONE

KNOCK THRICE FOR LUCK

THREE KNOCKS ON WOOD WILL BRING YOU GOOD FORTUNE ALL DAY LONG

MIND YOUR PINS AND NEEDLES

FOR FEAR OF IGNITING THE FLAMES OF A QUARREL
YOU MUST NEVER MAKE A GIFT OF A PIN TO A GOOD FRIEND

LEND THEM ONE FOR NINTY-NINE YEARS IF YOU MUST
BUT ONLY IF YOU MUST · YET NEVER AS A GIFT

MIND THAT YOUR SHOES
REMAIN ON THE GROUND

BAD LUCK · STRONG STORMS · DEATH
MAY FOLLOW IF YOUR SHOES TREAD WHERE THEY DO NOT BELONG
TROUBLE IN YOUR MARRIAGE · STUTTERING AS AN ACTOR

KEEP YOUR SHOES ON THE GROUND WHERE THEY BELONG

A MOST FORTUNATE ENCOUNTER!
THE BLACK CAT!

FORETELLS OF A SUCCESSFUL PERFORMANCE WHEN FOUND IN A THEATRE
ENSURES A SAFE RETURN FROM THE SEA WHEN KEPT IN THE HOME
GIVE YEARS OF HAPPINESS WHEN GIVEN TO THE BRIDE ON HER WEDDING DAY
MEANS MONEY IS COMING YOUR WAY WHEN FOUND SITTING ON YOUR STOOP

HOKHOKU

BRITISH COLUMBIA ∗ CANADA

Our minds are capable of subconsciously determining the height, width and size of a given object, based on our existing knowledge of other things that we see near it. But what happens when we look into the sky? Without a point of reference, it's practically impossible to determine the size of objects overhead. This optical imparity is exactly the advantage that the Hokhoku needs to secure its prey.

Soaring overhead, the Hokhoku enters our vision as the dark shadow of the common raven. It rises and falls overhead, a black streak against the cobalt sky, and we barely give it a second thought. And this is the moment the Hokhoku attacks. As it begins its descent, it becomes clear that this isn't a common raven after all – the bird is enormous, getting larger and larger until coal-black feathers eclipse the sky, and all at once you feel sharp talons sink into your flesh.

Preferring the meat of humans to that of other, less intelligent creatures, the Hokhoku will attack even the scrawniest of people before it turns to horses and livestock. Taking great joy in playing with its food, the Hokhoku viciously toys with its prey before killing it – ascending rapidly, arching high in the sky, then repeatedly dropping and catching its snack, sometimes passing it from one claw to another in midair.

The Hokhoku rarely kills with its great talons. Instead, the kill strike is efficiently delivered by its obsidian, thick and slightly curved beak – hard as good steel, and made for breaking and crunching bones and cracking human skulls.

The Hokhoku considers the eyes and brains of humans to be nourishing delicacies. In some cases, it will only consume the brain, leaving the rest of the body for scavengers to feast on.

Lucky is the prey that is eaten on the spot, even after being toyed with, for at least the end comes quickly with a proficient blow. Less fortunate targets are carried off to nests high in the mountains where they are given, still alive, to the Hokhoku's young, who, unskilled in killing prey, will clumsily tear at their victim's flesh, painfully prolonging their demise.

Since the first ships landed on the eastern coast, the history of North America has been a tale of humankind's attempts to tame wild lands. But stray even just ten meters from a wilderness trail, and you might find out just how fierce nature can be.

Deep in the wood, where the forest meets water, the Pukubts makes his home. Built out of decomposing logs and moss-covered bark, it is so well hidden under the dense canopy that some believe that the Pukubts is invisible. It is here that the Wildman of the Wood, the King of Ghosts, lives with the spirits of those who have drowned, feasting on cockles and waiting for another lost wanderer to cross his path.

He is a small being – diminutive, lean, sinewy and rawboned – and the bent and malnourished structure of his skeletal frame is easily seen through his skin, which is murky green and dark as the foliage that surrounds him. His face is gaunt and angular, his long, pointed nose sinks toward his upper lip. The Pukubts' eyes are round and pale, and seem to glow slightly in the darkness, reflecting even the slightest illumination that is directed toward them. The collection of souls that he has accumulated hover about him as he makes his way through the wood.

His life in isolation has made him uneasy around people, but in the darkness of his wood, the Pukubts still seeks humans out. If he happens to find you wandering in the forest alone, lost or stranded, he may offer you some sustenance from a cockle-shell plate. What looks to be dried salmon and wild berries is in reality a type of ghost food – a combination of rotting wood and the rancid, maggoty flesh of lizards and snakes. If you eat what he offers, your soul will become his, and you will be cursed into hovering alongside the Pukubts, wandering the forest forever. Tormented with hunger and anguish, you will be tasked with dispersing his malevolence onto any human who dares to venture into the darkness of the forest.

Some believe that the Pukubts' intent is simply to ensure that the wild places of the world remain wild. He stands as a reminder that not all the earth should belong to humankind.

⟶⟨⟩ OGOPOGO ⟨⟩⟵

BRITISH COLUMBIA * CANADA

The Secwépemc and Syilx peoples were the first to live on the shores of the ancient and deep Okanagan Lake. For centuries, they knew of the danger that resided in its waters.

Naitaka, the spirit of the lake, lived in a cave in the waters near Rattlesnake Island, and was known to possess an immense amount of power alongside a foul disposition. He sometimes took the shape of a large serpent, 70 feet long, with the diameter of a large tree. To cross Okanagan's waters safely, Naitaka demanded a blood offering. For hundreds of years, the First Nations would sacrifice small animals on the shore before entering the water, knowing Naitaka could use his long tail to conjure up fierce storms and rough waters to drown those who offended him.

Chief Timbasket, a proud man who visited the area, refused to offer a sacrifice to Naitaka, for his arrogance would not allow him to admit the existence of such a creature. He entered Okanagan in a canoe, accompanied by his family. He sat proudly in the stern of the boat, rowing slowly and methodically across the calm lake. All was well, until suddenly the surface began to churn, swirls of water dancing around the canoe whipped up into a torrent, and in an instant, they were gone – the canoe, Chief Timbasket and his whole family – all sucked to the bottom of the lake in a massive maelstrom.

In the mid-1800s, John MacDougall, a settler in the area, was crossing the lake as he had done many times before, with his horses tied up and swimming behind his canoe. As he approached the western shore, the horses began to get agitated and unsettled. As the water thrashed around them, one by one the horses were all pulled under. Acting immediately, he was able to cut the boat's rope just before he and his canoe met the same fate.

Sightings have continued over the years, although encounters have become less common. Some believe that with the arrival of European settlers to the region, Naitaka, now known as Ogopogo, has all but disappeared. That being said, Okanagan is the deadliest lake in British Columbia for drownings, so perhaps Naitaka simply waits for the food to find him, rather than revealing himself in order to catch his prey.

BE AWARE
LAKE MONSTER!

KEEP CHILDREN AND SMALL PETS CLOSE TO SHORE

MIND YOUR SURROUNDINGS

LISTEN FOR LOUD SLAPPING ON THE WATER'S SURFACE

BEWARE THE QUIET WATERS FLOWING OVER DEEP POOLS

UNKNOWN TERRORS LURK BENEATH

VESSELS UPENDED · PULLED UNDER · SUNK · VIOLENTLY CAPSIZED

SWIM AT ONE'S OWN RISK

MEANDER NOT THROUGH THE MURKY DEPTHS OF THE ALDER GROVE IN
WHICH THE OPHIDIAN FIEND RESIDES, SLINKING IN ITS BRACKISH
SHALLOWS, LUNGING WITH POISONED MOUTH AND CUSPIDATED TEETH

MAKE AN OFFERING BEFORE YOU CROSS

TOBACCO · WILD RICE · HERBS · BLOOD FROM YOUR FRESHLY SLICED HAND

THE DEVIL'S ISLAND GIANT

MANITOBA * CANADA

At the southern end of Lake Winnipeg sits a tiny speck of land known as Devil's Island. It is a popular ice-fishing spot during the short days of winter, and at night it is frequented by timber wolves scavenging the undesirable small fish left behind.

One evening, an Icelandic immigrant named Jonas decided to test his skill at hunting the wolves. The moon hung low and bright in the sky as he hitched up his dogs and started out over the frozen lake, but as he reached the island, clouds began to roll in. It was still light enough to hunt, but by midnight, and with no wolves in sight, the moon was completely obscured. Instead of traveling home in the dark, he decided to bunk down in a small, deserted cabin just outside the ghost town of Welsh Harbor. The smell of dust and old fish hung in the cabin's air, and Jonas made fast work of setting up his bedding. Sleep came quickly.

An hour or two later, Jonas was woken by a loud and incessant knocking on the door and walls. Some of his dogs howled and lunged at the air, while others cowered in the corner, yelping and whining in fear. He leapt to his feet, grabbed his gun, and prepared to stand against whatever came through the door. After much commotion, the door at last burst open and a great arm and hand reached in. Pandemonium erupted as the hand ransacked the cabin as if rummaging through a box. Jonas fell to the ground in terror, while the dogs leapt and gnashed at the long, sinewy fingers until eventually, seemingly satisfied, the gargantuan hand grabbed Jonas's fur bedding and then retreated as suddenly as it had arrived.

With the door open, Jonas stood in the threshold, gun in hand, peering into the night. His dogs growled quietly, hackles raised, as they paced back and forth around their master.

It wasn't until sunlight crested the horizon that Jonas let down his guard. He wondered what type of tracks this creature might have left, but when he looked, he found nothing – no trail, no footprint, no handprint, nothing at all. There was no evidence that anyone other than he and his dogs had been at the cabin the previous night.

⚜ THE FLAMING BRIDE ⚜
OF BANFF SPRINGS HOTEL
ALBERTA * CANADA

There are a few days in each of our lives, important days, when our emotions are at their highest, and our senses at their most acute. It must have been such a day as this when a young bride, whose name has been lost to both time and lore, married the man she loved. As evening approached, she prepared herself to celebrate the best day of her young life in the ballroom of the Banff Springs Hotel.

She was the only daughter of a wealthy lumber baron, and her wedding had been billed as the social event of the new century. No expense had been spared on this opulent party, which included a lavish dinner and reception at the Banff Springs Hotel. The bride wore a wide dress with many layers of crinoline, to fulfil her desire of looking as though she was gliding down the long winding staircase. Oh, and what a staircase it was! Grand and constructed of marble, it gave onto a breathtaking vista of the Canadian Rockies. For this special occasion, the stairs were lined with candles, and hundreds of small flames illuminated the hall in a golden hue.

At the foot of the stairs stood her groom. As the bride took her first step, their eyes locked, and the two held each other's gaze as she continued her descent. She paused for a moment on the first landing, briefly taking in the entirety of the room, perhaps to savor the moment, or to take a snapshot in her mind to save as a lifelong memory. As she continued walking down the stairs, the bride's gown billowed slightly, hardly noticeable, but just enough to brush against one of the candles. A short flash of illumination preceded the firestorm of her gown bursting into flame.

As she stumbled forward trying to escape the inferno that had begun to engulf her, she lost her balance and, as if in a great Pagan ritual, she began to roll down the stairs as a great wheel of flame, breaking her neck along the way. What had been a moment of such intense joy was in an instant turned into unimaginable anguish, as her groom threw his coat over his new bride's charred and broken body to help put out the fire. When the flames were finally extinguished, her lifeless body lay smoldering at the foot of the stairs.

Years later, guests of the hotel began to report seeing a woman in a white wedding gown make her way down to the first landing of the stairway before dissipating into a faint mist, as if caught in a light breeze. Others have called the front desk to report the sound of weeping coming from the bridal suite, only to be told that no one is staying there. From time to time, guests have asked who the young bride dancing by herself in the ballroom is, and have wondered if there was a wedding being held at the hotel.

The most horrifying claims come from those who have the misfortune to be staying at the hotel around the anniversary of the bride's tragic demise. Those guests claim that as the bride walks down the stairs, her gown appears to burst into flame, yet she continues her descent, her body bending and cracking as it becomes more misshapen and deformed until, on the very last step, she releases a bloodcurdling shriek before vanishing into a burst of frigid air.

·᪳᪳ MÎMÎKWÎSIWAK ᪳᪳·

MANITOBA * CANADA

The Laurentian Plateau is a massive slab of ancient rock which forms the core of the North American continent. Hidden in the crevices of the hard rock here, a race of little people make their home.

No more than 20 inches tall, the Mîmîkwîsiwak (Ma-ma-kwa-se-wak) are a diminutive yet strong species. As ancient as the rock itself, they are masters of crafting stone. After generations of living mainly underground in the darkness, their eyes have become enlarged and widely spaced. Their broad, round heads are slit by gaping grins; their thin lips pulled taut reveal mouths full of jagged, needle-sharp teeth. Their limbs, long and lean, are inconceivably powerful. An earnest and purposeful people, they are proud of, and watchful over, the land they have claimed as their own.

For many decades there was peace between the Mîmîkwîsiwak and the tribes who lived near them. Over the years, they even traded with one another – the Mîmîkwîsiwak provided arrowheads, stone tools and hammers to tribes, who in return gave them dried meats, medicine and sweet maple syrup. As time passed, however, the tribes learned to fend for themselves, and they began to rely less and less on the Mîmîkwîsiwak – some even forgot the little people existed.

The Mîmîkwîsiwak lived easily without what they had been given in trade. However, the other tribes' incursions onto their land without acknowledgment was seen as a deliberate provocation. Irritation quickly gave way to resentment, and what had once been a relationship based on trust and understanding became riddled with doubt and intolerance. Small acts of mischief by the Mîmîkwîsiwak worsened from ripping holes in the tribes' fishing nets and triggering hunting snares to stealing the meat, medicine and food that had at one time been traded with them. As the thefts became more frequent, the Mîmîkwîsiwak also became more brazen, regularly taking small children who were left unattended.

All along the ridge of the Laurentian Plateau, from far north in Canada, all the way down to the American Plains, you can find the Mîmîkwîsiwaks' warnings – petroglyphic symbols of soured kindness. Be advised to pay heed to these cautions, walk vigilantly on these lands, and pray that the petroglyphs are all you see of the Mîmîkwîsiwak.

·❀· THE SKULL-FACED BISHOP ·❀·

BRITISH COLUMBIA * CANADA

The gold rush of the mid-1800s saw over a hundred thousand people make the trek to the Yukon gold fields of northwest Canada and Alaska. Fort Victoria, which had been established as a fur trading post, became the first stop on the trail north. Although many just passed through on their way to strike it rich, thousands of less adventurous opportunists settled at the fort, turning the small outpost into to the burgeoning city of Victoria almost overnight. Businesses of all kinds popped up to support the needs of the prospectors – taverns, outfitters, food suppliers, brothels and, eventually, places of worship.

In 1863, a priest from Belgium, Father Charles-Jean Seghers, was one of the first to make the arduous journey to Fort Victoria. He was a handsome young man, and despite being only 24 years old, he made quick work of building up a congregation. Although he only had clapboard and canvas to work with, he soon established a Catholic church, and within ten years, he was named Bishop of the Diocese of Vancouver Island.

Having created a Catholic foothold in Victoria, Bishop Seghers set his aspirations on a more ambitious task: "spreading the Divine Savior's gospel among the North American heathen." The bishop, along with two Jesuit priests, Pascal Tosi and Aloysius Robaut, a layman called Frank Fuller, and a French-Canadian laborer whose name is not recorded, set out overland to Alaska, as Bishop Seghers was determined to reach the remote Indigenous villages of the Yukon Territories before the Protestants. When the group started the long trek down the Yukon River, Fuller began to act strangely. He said he could hear voices, and would have long conversations, and sometimes arguments, with himself. He began to claim that he thought his companions were planning to kill him. One day, following an argument with Fuller, the French-Canadian laborer disappeared. The priests thought perhaps Fuller's increasingly erratic behavior had driven the laborer to leave the expedition and head for home, so they continued without him.

When they came to the confluence of the Yukon and Stewart rivers, Bishop Seghers proposed that the two Jesuit priests continue up the Stewart River, while he and Fuller continued down the Yukon River to Nulato, spreading God's message en route. Reluctantly, Tosi and Robaut agreed.

The bishop and Fuller, along with two Indigenous guides, carried on along the Yukon, with Fuller becoming more and more erratic as the days passed. They stopped at a small fish camp to rest up before making the final push down river. Bishop Seghers was in good spirits, happy that he'd make it to Nulato well ahead of the Anglicans.

The following morning, the party readied themselves for the last leg of their year-long journey. As the bishop bent down to pick up his pack, a frantic Fuller fired a single shot through his heart, killing Seghers instantly. With a great sigh, Fuller holstered his gun, and told the horrified guides that it had been necessary to kill the bishop, but he didn't explain why. The guides carefully wrapped the bishop's body and continued on to Nulato, with Fuller still accompanying them and the corpse in tow.

It was in the depths of a bitterly cold Yukon winter when news of the bishop's death made its way to Tosi and Robaut. With the rivers frozen and the overland routes snowed in, the two priests would have to wait until the spring thaw to travel north and collect the bishop's body. Although it had been kept in an icehouse for preservation, by the time the priests arrived in Nulato, rodents had consumed most of the bishop's face. There, wrapped in waxed canvas, was not the handsome young man they had once known, but instead a horrifying, grimacing skull-faced reminder of the harshness of the North American wilds. The bishop's body was taken to Victoria where it was interned in the newly constructed St Andrew's Cathedral.

It wasn't long before strange sightings began in the cathedral. Parishioners and priests alike reported seeing translucent shadows of a solitary man strolling about the grounds, hands clasped behind his back. There were reports of the same man stepping into the confessional, where, upon investigation, the stall was always empty. The clergy attempted to keep these accounts quiet, but in time, the apparition took on an entirely different appearance, as if to say, "I am here, you will see me."

Fully dressed in bishop's attire, the figure still glides in the shadows of St Andrew's Cathedral. He stands in the alcoves, staring out over the congregation, hands held at his waist, his face mostly obscured except for his wide, toothy grin. Vacant yet rueful, it's an expression that immediately evokes a sense of melancholy. As one's eyes adjust to the light, it becomes apparent that this is the fleshless smirk of a bare-boned skull – the faceless spirit of Victoria's first bishop.

PROSPECTOR LORE

NEVER HARM A CAMP ROBBER!

THOUGH THEIR SONG IS LOUD, THOUGH THEY STEAL YOUR FOOD AND SHINY
THINGS, THOUGH THEY FLIT AND FLUTTER IN FLOCKS A-PLENTY, NEVER
CURSE A CAMP ROBBER. NEVER SWAT NOR SWING AT THEIR JITTERED FLIGHT,
NEVER CAST A STONE NOR HARM A SINGLE FEATHER OF THEIR WING.

► TO KILL THIS BIRD MEANS NO MORE GOLD ◄

ALWAYS PUT THE RIGHT GLOVE ON FIRST

NEVER WEAR YOUR SHIRT BACKWARD
NOR YOUR SOCKS INSIDE OUT

MIND YOUR TOOLS

► NEVER LEND OUT YOUR GOLD PAN ◄
UNLESS YOU AIM TO GIVE AWAY YOUR LUCK

A STANDING TOOL WELCOMES AN UNSEEN HAND
► LAY DOWN YOUR PICK AND HAMMER AT THE END OF THE DAY ◄

NEVER SPEND YOUR LUCKY COIN • NOR TAKE A TWO-DOLLAR BILL

THE DEUCE IS THE DEVIL'S NAME AND ONLY BAD LUCK WILL FOLLOW
IF IT MUST BE TAKEN
TEAR OFF THE LOWER LEFT CORNER OF THE BILL

·····⚜ THE GICHIGAMI GOONCH ⚜·····

MINNESOTA ✴ UNITED STATES

Flowing between the Twin Ports of Superior, Wisconsin and Duluth, Minnesota, the Saint Louis River lazily empties into Lake Superior. Once wild, concrete and rebar have softened its shores and dredging has calmed its rapids. But the urban growth, excessive traffic and years of industry of these two cities have also poisoned the river waters and contaminated its sediment. By the mid-twentieth century, the Saint Louis River was the most polluted waterway in both states.

This manmade evolution to an urban waterway has not entirely pacified the once wild river. As humans have harnessed the technology to tame it, a more savage development has occurred, one which is instinctively aggressive, fearless, and made of flesh, bone and sharp teeth. Lurking among the mucky sediment of the riverbed, feeding for decades on poisoned fish and human refuse, a monster has slowly grown. Nearly twenty-five feet long, covered not in scales, but smooth almost translucent skin. The creature's mouth cuts across the entirety of its body, a wide gaping slit full of row after row of jagged sharp teeth. Its eyes, as big as hubcaps, are highly developed for sight in silty waters of the Saint Louis, but it's the creatures barbels – like a cat's whiskers – that are its most developed sense. Part fingers, part tongue they sweep the darkness both feeling and tasting for something edible.

Riding the warm currents of the Saint Louis as it belches waste and toxins into the frigid waters of Lake Superior, the Goonch prowls the waters, ever searching for larger prey. Although too cold for even the hardiest of swimmers, these clear waters attract scuba divers from all over the world wanting to explore their mysterious depths. This monster does not discriminate, it doesn't mind what kind of flesh satiates it – human or animal, it matters not. The Goonch only knows that when it senses movement, some kind of meal is present. Violently twisting its massive head, it jerks open its mouth, sucking water, diver, tanks and all into the vacuum created by its gaping maw. Dragged over razor-sharp teeth and through the bone-crushing constriction of the creature's esophagus, the diver is carried into the Goonch's belly. As if this isn't terrifying enough, with sufficient oxygen in their tank, it is possible that a diver could survive miserably for an hour or two, before eventually taking their last breaths in the acidic stomach of the Gichigami Goonch.

-ᕽᑓᔦᕽ THE FABLE OF LA CORRIVEAU ᕽᑓᔦᕽ-

QUEBEC * CANADA

Marie-Josephte was a spirited young girl. As her parents' only surviving child, she had a solitary upbringing with little instruction. She spent hours and days, weeks and months exploring the wilderness of New France. Meandering unaccompanied through the woods, she began to dabble in the dark arts and diablerie, but when, at the age of 16, her parents wanted to marry her off to an older man, she was incapable of using these skills to escape her fate.

Perhaps because she had married so young, or perhaps because her wild spirit could not settle for a man whom she had not chosen herself, Marie-Josephte's mind, and heart, began to stray. One night, she plied her husband with strong ale and good food. When he fell asleep at the table, she melted some lead over the fire and poured it into his ear. He died and Marie-Josephte got away with the murder.

Her second husband was a handsome man, but despite being in love, Marie-Josephte's eyes began to wander again. One evening she grabbed a hatchet, and after several blows to the back of her husband's head, her second marriage was over.

This time the murder was too obvious, and Marie-Josephte was arrested, found guilty and sentenced to death. On a beautiful spring day, she was hanged for her heinous deed. As a warning to anyone else tempted to break the law in what was now the Province of Quebec, Marie-Josephte's body was placed in a gibbet and dangled from a tall, wooden stake at a busy crossroads near the south shore of the Saint Lawrence River.

This spectacle of the macabre quickly became extremely grim – ravens and rats, flies and maggots made a meal of her. The sight of a decaying body and the stench of purified flesh deterred folks from passing her way, yet no one removed the foul corpse.

Soon, strange happenings started – Marie-Josephte's emaciated and rawboned hands began to reach out toward passersby as she whispered their names. The citizens of Quebec took matters into their own hands, and in the dark of night, a group of brave men pulled her down, and hastily buried her deep in unconsecrated ground.

Although she had been laid to rest, Marie-Josephte's hauntings continued, and her corpse began to rise nightly to torment those who traveled the south shore of the Saint Lawrence.

Late one night, François Dubé, a farmer, passed the place where Marie-Josephte's body had once hung. He removed his cap and crossed himself while saying a brief prayer. As he whispered "Amen," he heard a click-clacking noise behind him that seemed to be getting closer. He pressed his horse to pick up her pace as the sounds of snapping bones and dragging chains closed in. He dared to look behind him just in time to see the shriveled corpse of Marie-Josephte, still encased in her gibbet, climbing into his wagon.

As the scent of damp earth and rot enveloped him, he felt her leathered hands clasp his neck, and the two of them fell from the carriage onto the ground. Boney fingers dug into his flesh as sodden, coarse hair swept over his face. Rancid cold breath brushed his cheek as a ragged voice choked out, "Take me across the river, Dubé." Lost souls cannot cross flowing water alone, so Marie-Josephte needed him.

Dubé refused. "I will strangle you!" she threatened, as dirt and maggots fell onto Dubé's face. "I'll squeeze the life from you and ride your soul across to l'Île-d'Orléans." Dubé, to his own detriment, once again refused her. She strangled him on the spot, and, as promised, rode his good soul over the river to the island that her spirit still haunts.

It is said that on windy nights you can hear the click-clack cracking of her bones, and that gusts carry her cackle and wails. On the light evening breeze of spring, you can hear her laughter as she sits astride his restless soul, pressing him onward: "Ya-ya, Dubé, ya-ya."

SPELLCASTERS AND TRICKSTERS WERE SEEN AS A THREAT TO THEIR COMMUNITY
SPEAKING IN RIDDLES AND TURNING WORDS TO INCITE DISCORDANCE

SORCIÈRES D'ACADIE

◄ WITCHES ɪɴ ACADIA ►

Life in the colonies was not easy, reliance on one's neighbors and the strength of the community was paramount to one's survival. Those who chose to go it alone were commonly misunderstood and viewed with suspicion.

SPINSTERS ᴀɴᴅ HERMITS ᴀɴᴅ SOLITUDINARIANS

IT WAS UNCOMMON AND EVEN SUSPICIOUS TO LIVE ON ONE'S OWN IN THE NEW WORLD
THOSE WHO LIVING ON THE EDGES OF CIVILIZATION WERE CONSIDERED DANGEROUS
EVEN WORSE YET IF YOU CHOSE TO LIVE AS A SOLITARY WOMAN

ONLY THROUGH A PACT WITH THE DEVIL

❧ SEULEMENT GRÂCE ❧ À UN PACTE AVEC LE DIABLE

UNLIKE MANY OTHER SOCIETIES' BELIEFS ABOUT WITCHES, THE ACADIANS BELIEVED
YOU COULD ONLY GAIN THE ABILITY TO CAST SPELLS BY MAKING A PACT WITH SATAN

➤ YOUR ETERNAL SOUL WILLFULLY GIVEN IN RETURN FOR EARTHLY GIFTS ◄

THE INDIGENOUS PEOPLE OF NEW FRANCE

GODLESS IN THE EYES OF THE CHRISTIAN COLONISTS, INDIGENOUS PEOPLE WERE SEEN NOT ONLY AS DEVIL WORSHIPERS, BUT QUITE OFTEN AS DEMONS AND DEVILS THEMSELVES. THE COLONISTS BELIEVED THAT INDIGENOUS PEOPLE WORSHIPED THE WILDS OF THE LAND, AND ACTIVILY TEMPTED THE COLONISTS TO RETURN TO THE WILDERNESS.

THE TRUE STORY OF
MARIE-JOSEPHTE CORRIVEAU

NINE SIBLINGS

SHE WAS THE ONLY SURVIVING CHILD OF A FAMILY OF NINE CHILDREN
AND SHE WAS MARRIED OFF AT THE AGE OF SIXTEEN

HUSBAND NO. 1: CHARLES BOUCHARD

HER FIRST HUSBAND WAS NEARLY TEN YEARS OLDER THAN HER
THEY WERE MARRIED FOR ELEVEN YEARS AND HAD THREE CHILDREN
HE DIED IN 1760 OF NATURAL CAUSES

HUSBAND NO. 2: LOUIS ÉTIENNE DODIER

A YEAR LATER MARIE-JOSEPHTE MARRIED LOUIS
A MEAN AND SPITEFUL MAN, ABUSIVE TO BOTH HER AND HER CHILDREN
AS WELL AS ANY OTHER ANIMAL OR CREATURE IN HIS CUSTODY
HE WAS FOUND DEAD LESS THAN THREE YEARS AFTER THEY WED
KICKED TO DEATH BY HIS HORSE

A TRIAL A SENTENCE AN EXECUTION A PREVARICATION •

In the public opinion, Marie-Josephte was guilty even before her trial began, but after a tribunal officially declared her guilty she was sentenced to hang for the murder. In addition to execution, she was also found guilty of treason (due to the fact that, in the colony, a wife was considered her husband's lesser) and was sentenced to exposure – public display in a metal gibbet. Her corpse hung in its gibbet at a crossroads for two months, before what little remained of her was buried, gibbet and all, outside of the Christian cemetery wall. Over the years, her small wooden marker disintegrated, and her grave was lost to both time and the elements.

FANNING THE FLAMES OF INFAMY

In 1851, Marie-Josephte's grave was rediscovered during a construction project. There was little more than the iron gibbet left, which fed into the legend that had evolved over the decades since her death. It was cleaned up and stored in the church basement. When the gibbet was stolen, this only added fuel to the fire of the infamy of la corriveau.

⸻⁂ SASQUATCH ⁂⸻

PACIFIC NORTHWEST

The men had made their way to the hunting cabin, miles off the beaten path and far into the wilds of the Snoqualmie. September in the Cascades of Washington meant warm days but cold nights, and as darkness was upon them, they quickly went about building a fire to cut through the evening chill. The small rustic cabin was without electricity or heat; there was a shallow porch that wrapped around three sides, with the fourth side facing the wilderness. Two small windows on each side, along with a door on the front of the building offered some natural light. After setting up their bedrolls and eating a quick meal, the four men relaxed on the porch with some whiskey and cigars, and enjoyed the quiet solitude of the mountain wilderness.

The four of them were old friends, and this would be their seventh hunt together. After a dram or two, the jocular comradery could not have been any more palpable. The night went on and a cloudless sky opened to the brilliance of the cosmos – stars and planets shown in all their glory. The Milky Way sliced through the southwest sky, and an eerie quiet hung over the wood. One by one the men retired for the night, until at last only one remained alone in the darkness – merry from the whiskey, he closed his eyes to savor the silence of the wilderness. Out from the darkness, a low grunt broke the peace. Heavy footsteps skittered from another direction as a long, low howl rang out through the night. The man's eyes were wide open as more guttural cries followed from all directions, and more movement could be heard throughout the forest.

As he stood frozen on the front step, the wood fell silent again. An avid hunter, he felt he knew this feeling, strange as it was, and he could only assume this must have been how an elk felt just before it fell prey to his rifle. He could feel a gaze watching him from the darkness.

Ca-clank! a large object stuck the metal roof. Ka-ging! then another. The three other men in the cabin were awoken by the noise and came to the door as the fourth man clambered to get in. What followed was a great volley of stones and sticks descending from the forest, ricocheting and skittering off the roof and walls of the cabin, followed by a cacophony of hoots and howls and low, guttural grunts. Loud knocks rang out through the cabin, created by what sounded like large hands banging on the walls.

For fifteen long minutes it seemed as if the entire wilderness had come alive to assault the men. And then, just as quickly as it had begun, the forest fell back to silence and the wilderness retreated, but not without delivering one final warning as a last stone fell loudly on the metal roof.

The fire was stoked, lanterns were lit, and no more whiskey was consumed that night. The following morning, the men packed up their bedrolls and rifles, cigars, whiskey and beef jerky and headed back toward civilization. As they hastily made their way out of the front door and across the shallow porch they all saw them, but none dared call attention to them – footprints, 19, maybe 20 inches long, tens of them in the soft dirt circling the cabin, and then there were the handprints. On the siding of the cabin were hundreds of handprints, each roughly a foot wide and ten feet off the ground. The men quickly made their way through the thick wood, sticking only to known paths. They kept their eyes low so that they wouldn't see what was stalking them in the shadows.

§◦⁓—⁓◦§

The name Sasquatch comes from the Salish word *se'sxac* which translates to "wild men," however stories of these creatures come from all over North America. While the names and traditions differ, the descriptions remain fairly consistent – a large, hairy, humanlike, bipedal creature, with broad shoulders, a minimal neck, and long arms. Its coloring ranges from deep black to dark brown or reddish hair, and where skin is visible it is of a similar hue. A conservative estimate of a Sasquatch's height is around nine feet, though some people claim to have seen some creatures as large as fifteen feet tall. Some say that a Sasquatch's eyes glow yellow or orange when struck with torchlight. And then there's the scent – they all seem to smell distinctly musky, much like rotten eggs and damp earth.

Those who have encountered these beings often claim that they sensed they were being stalked before seeing their stalker. Often assuming it was some other large carnivore, they typically readied themselves for a run in with a bear or a cougar, but soon realized they were being tracked by a creature perhaps more curious than hungry, more cautious than a common predator, and much more capable of sustained concealment.

Typically in modern encounters, the Sasquatch uses the darkness of night to make its presence known, throwing large rocks and sticks to cause unusual noise, as well as making audible calls, hoots and howls, low grunts and high-pitched screams. Usually, a Sasquatch means no harm and keeps its distance while testing the will of those it stalks, but on occasion it'll steal food, meat or fish, or violently destroy camps as if trying to remind those encroaching on its territory about the true nature of the wilderness.

Some of the earliest known depictions of Sasquatch are located at Painted Rock, on the Tule River Reservation in California. Petroglyphs created by the Indigenous Yokuts some 500 to 1,000 years ago depict an image of a large man, known as the "hairy man." In addition to this glyph is another that depicts a group of hairy giants referred to as the "family," which suggest the presence of female and child Sasquatch-like creatures as well.

The Lummi of the coastal Pacific Northwest speak of the shy Ts'emekwes, who roamed the forests by day and kept their distance from the tribe. They also tell of another more threatening version of the beast named Stiyaha or Kwi-kwiyai, a dangerous, aggressive creature of the night who sometimes hunted humans for food. Children were warned not to say their names out loud, to prevent them from being carried off and killed. The Iroquois tell tales of a hair-covered giant with rock-hard skin known as Ot-ne-yar-heh ("Stone Giant"), who was aggressive and territorial in nature and was to be avoided at all times for fear of death.

Even as the Spanish explored and settled further north into what is now California, they wrote of "*los Vigilantes Oscuros*," the Dark Watchers. Creatures of unusual size and hairiness that stalked them by day and attacked late at the night, stealing their cattle and destroying their camps.

The most famous encounter of all was in 1958 in Humboldt County, California. Jerry Crew, a bulldozer driver working for a logging company in the wilderness of Six Rivers National Forest, discovered 16-inch human-like footprints set deep in the mud. Several of his coworkers also claimed to have seen similar tracks. They began to use the moniker "Bigfoot." Talk being as it is, the stories soon spread, and when additional strange incidents began to occur, such as a 450-pound oil drum moving without explanation, the local media began to take notice. First the *Humboldt Times* published an image of Jerry holding a plaster cast of one of the enormous footprints, soon followed by the *Los Angeles Times*. By late 1958 the story had run in almost every major newspaper in the United States, catapulting Sasquatch, aka Bigfoot, to a household name, and Northern California to the Bigfoot capital of the world.

SASQUATCH

A RANDOM CHRONICLE ᴼᶠ DOCUMENTED SIGHTINGS

History is full of first-hand accounts of seeing large, wild, hairy and massively strong creatures. From early Indigenous peoples, to the Europeans who settled across the continent, and even into modern times, humans have often found more than they expected to while exploring the wilds of North America.

◀ 1528: ALVAR NÚÑEZ CABEZA DE VACA – TEXAS ▶

Alvar Núñez Cabeza de Vaca found himself in the New World for the same reason as many other Spaniards – he wanted glory and wealth. He made the long and dangerous voyage across the Atlantic, but poor navigation skills and bad weather stranded Cabeza de Vaca and a handful of his men on the coast of what is now Texas, just north of the Spanish settlements of Mexico. While making the long trek down through the wilds of the southern Texas coast they encountered a large creature, nearly nine feet tall, covered in long reddish-brown hair, and capable of tearing a man limb from limb. In his diary, Cabeza de Vaca said he and his men called the creature Mala Cosa – vile creature.

◀ 1792: JOSE MARIANO MOZINO – NOOTKA SOUND ▶

During the English and Spanish exploration of the Northern Pacific Coast, a Spanish vessel sailed up an inlet that the Nootka people called Mowichat, now Nootka Sound. The young naturalist, Jose Mariano Mozino, took a fond interest in the Nootka's traditions, even venturing into the wild lands with them on several occasions. On one trip, he saw an animal that the tribe called "Matlog" – a huge creature, covered in coarse, black, bristly hair. Although its head resembled that of a human's, it was much larger, with a tall, broad forehead and a mouth full of sharp, bear-like fangs. The creature's strong arms seemed too long for the rest of its proportions, and its hairless hands were thick, with long black nails. It was said that the creature screamed and cried into the night like a great gathering of devils and demons.

🐾 1840: ELKANAH WALKER – WASHINGTON STATE 🐾

Elkanah Walker, a missionary to the Indigenous people near what is now modern-day Spokane, Washington. In his writings, he documented several stories about a race of hairy giants that inhabited the mountains to the east of his base. These giants were known to steal salmon from the fishing nets of the local Indigenous people at night, then eat the fish raw on the spot. Dangerous and cannibalistic, it was said that they also snuck into camps at night and kidnapped people in their sleep, running off into the darkness with full grown men under their arms. Those who were awake at the time of an attack knew the creatures were nearby due to their strong, nauseating scent. They also told of hearing the giants communicating with one another in the darkness with low grunts, high pitched screeches and whistles, while tossing stones into the village to see what moved.

🐾 1885: THE WILD GIRL OF CATAHOULA – LOUISIANA 🐾

In central Louisiana, over the span of almost a decade, there were sightings of a young woman who was fully naked, but covered from head to toe in black hair of varying lengths. The hair grew long from her head, then shorter from her shoulders, arms and legs. Her face and chest were mostly bare. She was once seen by two men fishing in a creek. They heard some hogs squealing in distress, and when they went to investigate, they came upon the wild girl standing with a dead pig under one arm, and what looked like a bloody knife in her other hand. They claimed she bared her teeth and released a blood-curdling cry before running off into the wood.

🐾 1924: APE CANYON – WASHINGTON STATE 🐾

Fred Beck, a gold prospector spotted a group of bears off in the distance, and decided to take shot at one of them with his rifle. To his horror, they all stood up, and after spotting him up the canyon, began to give chase, striding on two feet. Once safely back at the cabin, Beck and his fellow prospectors endured a night-long attack from the "gorilla men." Rocks pelted the walls and roof of the small cabin, as boulders crashed into the walls. The prospectors claimed that one of the creatures even thrust its hair-covered arm, its hand grabbing wildly at the air, through a window, and only withdrew when it was struck with a burning log. As the Sun rose, the creatures retreated back into the wood.

◈ 1924: ALBERT OSTMAN – BRITISH COLUMBIA ◈

Albert Ostman was sleeping near a burning fire when he was suddenly scooped up – sleeping bag and all – by a large Sasquatch, and was carried off into the night. Hauled over the Sasquatch's shoulder, Osman was carried up the side of a steep ravine and into the mountains where he was shown to three other creatures which he assumed were the Sasquatch's family. They dug through his belongings, and he claimed the younger Sasquatch even interacted with him, being particularly interested in a small tin and matches. Osman was held captive for just over a week, eating whatever he was given, and only escaped when the largest of the group of creatures took a large bite of his chewing tobacco and became unwell.

◈ 1937: MINING CAMP – SUPERSTITION MOUNTAINS, ARIZONA ◈

Near the edge of their camp, two prospectors were celebrating a profitable day of mining when one of their burros let out a terrifying bellow. When they arrived at the rope line it had been tied to, they saw a massive creature dragging off the poor animal's carcass, disappearing into the darkness before the men could even raise their guns. As large as a grizzly bear, they claimed the beast must have weighed around 500 pounds. It walked on its hind legs and stood about eight feet tall. Its coarse hair was matted and tangled, and the creature was filthy – it smelled of feces and rotten eggs. The two men spent the rest of the night with their fire blazing, wide awake and scared out of their wits.

◈ 1957: MICA MOUNTAIN – BRITISH COLUMBIA ◈

While out for a hike, a construction worker sat down for a mid-day meal. In the distance, he noticed a grizzly bear in a patch of low brush. With his rifle in hand, he decided to quietly observe the animal for a bit. To his surprise, the creature stood, and, walking on two legs, it strode boldly across the clearing. Nearly seven feet tall, the creature must have weighed around 300 pounds and was covered in dark brown, silver-tipped hair. The bare skin on its face, hands and chest was a dark, grayish brown, its arms were longer than a human's, and its neck was shorter and thicker. As it passed through the clearing it caught the man's scent, and stopped abruptly to look around until it caught sight of him. Staring for a moment, the creature turned and walked quickly in the other direction, looking over its shoulder once or twice to ensure it wasn't being followed.

◄ 1982: PAUL FREEMAN – THE BLUE MOUNTAINS, WASHINGTON ►

In 1982, a former US Forest Service Patrolman, Paul Freeman, found and cast the most convincing Sasquatch foot and hand prints ever seen. Forensic specialists at Washington State University documented that the casts were not only some of the most accurate in proportion, but that many of them also contained unique dermal ridges and skin whorls, similar to those you would find on many primates' hands and feet. These details make it seem unlikely that Freeman could have fabricated the prints.

◄ 2005: MICHAEL GREENE ►
UWHARRIE NATIONAL FOREST, NORTH CAROLINA

While camping solo in the nearly 50,000-acre Uwharrie National Forest, Greene, a former US Army tank commander heard the telltale sounds of something nearing his tent. Twigs snapped and leaves rustled, and suddenly something very large was looming over his tent. He heard a deafening roar before whatever had made the noise ran off into the night. The next day, some friends joined him, and with the comfort of companions, Greene brushed off the frightening occurrence of the previous night and they decided to stay in the same camp. The additional people must have helped keep the creature at a distance, as it didn't enter the camp again, however a few of the party claimed to have seen a large, eight-foot-tall ape-like creature lumbering about in the distance, striding along on two legs.

◄ 2019: MAYFLOWER GULCH – COLORADO ►

At 11,000 feet, a group of hikers taking a rest spotted a large, human-looking creature trying to scale a twenty-foot wall that was covered in ice and snow. They claimed the creature, which was covered in dark brown fur, was attempting to scurry up the wall but kept failing and falling back to the ground. They went to look for it, but when they arrived at the correct location, it was nowhere to be found. There were, however, several large foot and hand prints in the snow, and on the icy wall.

-❦❧ THE HEADLESS NUN ❦❧- OF FRENCH FORT COVE

NEW BRUNSWICK * CANADA

During the early years of colonization, the east coast of Canada saw the French and British locked in decades of conflict. One victory after another soon found the French colony of Acadia completely under British control. Some Acadians swore allegiance to their new king, some found themselves living through the harsh conditions of expulsion, and a brave few took to the Canadian wilds in the hope that that they might never be found.

News of the Acadians' struggle soon made its way back to France, to a young nun named Sister Marie Inconnue. She asked to be sent to the colonies to offer comfort to those in need, and she was put on the next available ship. She landed near an inlet known as French Fort Cove, where a small community of Acadians were sheltering.

Sister Marie quickly became a beloved member of the Acadian community, offering assistance where needed, supporting those who were ill and helping to feed the hungry. After a short time, however, word of an imminent British attack on the French Fort Cove Acadians spread through the community. Fearing that their valuables would soon become plunder, the Acadians gathered up all their money, jewelry, gold and silver and gave everything to Sister Marie for safe keeping. She set off alone, into the wilderness, and found a secluded place to bury the treasure.

Local thieves got wind of the buried valuables, and late one night, as Sister Marie was walking her usual path home after helping a patient, three assailants leapt out, pulled a burlap bag over her head and whisked her away to their hideout. Sister Marie resisted the thieves' questioning, never divulging the location of the treasure, but after hours of torture she finally succumbed to her ill treatment and died. The thieves were so disturbed by the horrifying expression on Sister Marie's face after her death, they lopped off her head and threw it into the sea. Her headless corpse was found by fishermen the following day.

The devastated Acadian community searched the cove and the wood surrounding it, but Sister Marie's head was never found. After a small local ceremony, her body was returned to France, where it was buried in a small cemetery near her old convent. Although her body was in France, her spirit

remained in New Brunswick, and Sister Marie continued the search for her missing head.

There were constant reports of nightly sightings of a dark figure, carrying a lantern, walking slowly and seemingly searching the edge of the path that Sister Marie had often taken. Some claimed the figure appeared to be wearing a nun's habit.

One night, as darkness was making its way through the wood, a local farmer was traveling the path home. He noticed a dim light ahead of him – a lantern – and took some comfort from the fact that there was another traveler on the path. As he got closer, however, his apprehension grew – he could see the figure more clearly, and recognized the distinct shape and pattern of a nun's habit. "*Coucou! Allô!*" he cried out nervously, but the nun walking ahead of him paid him no heed. He assumed she had not heard him, so as he approached he spoke again, "*Allô, bonsoir.*" As she slowly turned to face him, he saw that the nun had no head, and, filled with horror, he screamed and fell backward to the ground, grasping at the damp earth, clawing and kicking himself over root and stone. The headless nun thrust her lantern into the farmer's face as she bent down toward him, and with a voice fully audible, but hushed and soft as a whisper, she asked, "*Où est ma tête?*" ("Where is my head?"). The man stumbled to his feet and ran all the way back to the safety of his farm.

Although the Acadian settlement of French Fort Cove has since been abandoned, Sister Marie still searches the area for her missing head. Over the years, many have claimed to see a headless nun wandering the dense wood in the dead of night, and some say that she has asked them to help her look for it. One man says he once felt Sister Marie's ghostly hand reach out of the darkness to touch the back of his head, and claims that in the following days, three distinct, finger-sized patches of pure white hair began to grow – exactly where she touched him – among his dark amber hair.

If you choose to go out in search of Sister Marie Inconnue's spirit, be sure to bring a flashlight, and be sure, of course, to never go alone.

···❧ WENDIGO ❧···

GREAT LAKES REGION OF CANADA
AND THE UNITED STATES

The wendigo is winter's merciless spirit, the very manifestation of the brutality of the unrelenting north winds that grimly strip the horizon to bleakness, leaving behind a trail of desolation and famine. Driven by his gluttony and his desire to destroy and consume humans, the wendigo is always hungry, ever hunting, and is an insatiable, rapacious cannibal.

The spirit of the wendigo begins as a whisper on the cold winds during the cruelest months of winter's scarcity. It speaks to the weakest of people – those who feel they have been slighted, overlooked, or somehow given less – those who seek to balance their ledger at the cost of others'.

Preying on fear and a feeble mind, the wendigo feeds on the thoughts that most of us keep hidden. Once he finds a home there, his baneful presence begins to metastasize, jumping from one thought to another, one desire to the next, until he finally breaks his victim's will, possesses them completely, and incites action. Once the wendigo fully takes hold, hunger is ever present, and the temptation to feed on human flesh is unrelenting, finally manifesting as a famished rampage of murder and cannibalism. The more the wendigo eats, the larger it becomes, never finding a meal capable of fulfilling its hunger.

It is through cooperation and self-sacrifice that the wendigo is defeated – to stand up to its gnawing insistence, we must choose righteousness over greed. This is where we find the wendigo's greatest weakness. In the following story, we learn about an unlikely hero who is willing to give herself up to save her village.

❧·····❧

When the pot over the fire began to swing on its own, the old ones knew he was coming. Some sat in silence, some nervously fidgeted with their nightly tasks, and others seemingly stared at the emptiness before them, but all were contemplating their fate – they knew that no man or woman had ever defeated the wendigo. Few of them had noticed a young girl who sat by the fire, quietly stripping the bark from two sumac branches. It was only when she stood up and asked for a warm cup of tallow that the elders

realized she was dressed in preparation to face the depths of the bitter cold outside.

She threw open the door, and winter's cruelty was immediate. The frigid air tore its way into the girl's chest, the wind gnawing at what little of her skin was exposed. The deep snow beneath her squealed as it clawed and grabbed at her feet to slow her stride. Her dogs ran ahead to chase away the wendigo's dogs, whose yips and howls rose and fell in unison with the brutal north wind.

In the distance, the wendigo loomed giant against the horizon, striding effortlessly through the woods as his enormous hands brushed five, six and seven trees aside at once. His eyes were fixed on the smoke rising from the tiny village ahead as he made his way toward it.

When the little girl first saw the wendigo, her bravery did not waver. Indeed, she bore down even more, and as she ran across the frozen snow she began to grow. With each stride, she became a little taller, and when the two met in a clearing, the girl was only slightly shorter than the wendigo itself.

The wendigo snarled and howled as it sized her up. It gnashed its teeth, and the sound of shards of ice breaking soon turned to a low, gurgling cackle as his disbelief at the sight of such an unexpected opponent turned to amusement. The wendigo imagined its feast of human flesh as it lunged wildly and uncontrollably toward her. But as the wendigo rabidly swung his arms, the girl ducked and swayed. Reaching and grabbing, he lumbered awkwardly forward, missing his mark. He spun round, and in an attempted correction, lurched towards the girl once more. With a deft swing of one sumac branch, the girl landed a devastating blow to the wendigo's head, and a forceful whip of his leg with the other branch sent him tumbling to the ground, which was frozen as solid as the hardest granite, shattering the wendigo into a shower of icy shards upon impact. There, in the remnants, lay a gaunt man, emaciated and withered, with a broken skull.

The girl drank the warm tallow and returned to her normal size. She called to her dogs, who, brave and battered, licked her face, and circled her feet all the way back to the village. Her people welcomed her home a hero, and were forever honored that she was theirs.

⟶⟶ THE LAC WOOD SCREECHER ⟵⟵
QUEBEC * CANADA

Lac Wood lies deep in the wilds of northern Quebec, surrounded by dense woodland. A narrow footpath winds its way past fallen trees and lichen-covered boulders, a reminder of this land's unforgiving nature.

The Lac Wood Screecher makes this forest his home. We don't know what he looks like – no one who has ever laid eyes on him has been found alive – but that doesn't mean you won't know he's there. The sense of his presence begins with the eerie feeling of being watched and stalked. Things escalate when the wood falls nearly silent, save the sound of snapping twigs and breaking branches.

Wandering down the path, you'll find clumps of strange hair and dander on the ground and snagged in branches. Brushing against it will cause a prickling, crawling sensation and a persistent urge to scratch. With every itch, the irritation becomes more aggravated, intensifying into small red bumps and then a rash. If untreated, pustules can form, splitting and peeling the skin, causing infection.

As night falls and camps are made and fires are lit, the Screecher becomes more courageous. Sounding almost like a human mimicking animal noises, what begins as a low growl, raking and gravelly, morphs into loud whoops and shrill screams. The sounds circle the camp, seeming to come from throughout the forest. These penetrating assaults are deliberate, and are meant to cause bewilderment and confusion.

With each scream, your anxiety will rise, causing a stomach-churning sense of dread, until at once you will feel the inevitable urge to flee. Stumbling through the darkness, your heart pounding, your lungs will burn as branches, bushes and brambles tear at you.

A sound that starts as a low rasp and rises to an unholy, ear-splitting scream will bring you to your knees. Shivers will run up your spine as the screeching rises and falls, reverberating throughout the wood, its source's location impossible to determine. The bone-rattling cries will cause your head to throb and your nose to bleed, and nausea and vomiting will follow as your eardrums burst. Although the sound will now be muted, you will fall into convulsions from its violent vibrations, and these tremors will bend – and eventually break – your body, and turn your organs to mush.

THE BLACK HOUND
OF THE GREAT LAKES
GREAT LAKES REGION OF CANADA
AND THE UNITED STATES

The first ships passed between Lake Ontario and Lake Erie via the Welland Canal in 1829, and before long, more than a hundred ships a day were crossing from one lake to the other. The building of the canal was an amazing achievement – the engineers got their marvel and the banks and shipping companies got their financial triumph.

One of the ships that was traveling the canal had a crew of pranksters and rascals – every one of them was prone to devilry, mischievousness and, at times, utter wickedness. On this day, they had made it just over halfway through the crossing from Lake Ontario when the ship nearly ran up against the wall of the canal. As adjustments were made to correct its course, the vessel rolled a bit, but it was of no concern – the crew had seen much worse on open water. However, as the vessel jerked starboard, the ship's hound, a large, jet-black Newfoundland who patrolled the deck, was tossed into the turbulent waters. The fall was not fatal, but there was a shameful response from some of the men on deck. A few of them began to laugh as they watched the dog struggle to keep its head above water as the ship sailed on.

The dog's loyalty drove him to action. As the ship continued onward, the dog swam after it. Periodically he would catch up, but then he'd fall behind again, and the crew would jeer and guffaw. Despite this unkindness, the hound swam on. He had been a loyal companion for weeks aboard the ship, but the crew continued to mock him, until at last his struggle came to an end. As the ship forged ahead, the dog was pulled into the currents before being crushed between the closing gates of a lock. The ship's crew fell silent as the mass of crushed bone and flesh was overtaken by the rising water.

The ship cleared the canal and entered open water as night fell, and Lake Erie stretched out before them. Although the lake was calm, the evening was anything but – the night crew could hear what sounded like a struggling animal in the water just off the port side of the ship. They were nearly in the middle of the lake, and it seemed unlikely that any animal would be able to swim out so far. Stranger yet were the conscience-haunting sounds of a dog in distress, whimpers and heavy breathing from out over the water. Later in the night, the crew awoke to unearthly howls and the loud padding of heavy paws on deck. Those who investigated found nothing, first tracking the noise to the stern of the ship only to then hear the sound come from the bow. Once at the bow, the sound seemed to come from the stern again. The mournful wailing became more and more desperate through the early morning hours, and only ceased once the sun broke on the eastern horizon.

After docking in Cleveland the crew disbanded, but tales of the Black Hound of the Great Lakes lived on. In 1875, a ship called the *Isaac G. Jenkins* was crossing Lake Erie. It was a quiet night, there was a clear sky, and the water was calm. As a deckhand kept watch to ensure the vessel kept its course, he witnessed a strange sight. Out of the night's darkness, a black dog leapt over the port-side railing at the bow of the ship and proceeded to jaunt casually across the deck toward the starboard side. The beast stopped midway and looked directly at the sailor – a motionless interaction lasting only a moment – before turning and continuing on its course. Arriving at the starboard side of the vessel, it jumped the railing and was gone. There was no splash, no water on the deck to show that a wet dog had been there, in fact there was no trace of the animal at all.

The next morning, the sailor was in a frantic state. Not a single explanation for why he may have imagined a dog that was not there could calm him. His crew mates tried to convince him that he had merely seen the captain's dog, but this was to no avail, as he simply reasoned that the captain's dog – a black and white spaniel, not a Newfoundland – was still onboard.

After the sailor's repeated claims that the dog was a sign from the other side, the captain, fearing his crew would enter a state of mass hysteria, had no choice but to drop him off at the next port. The ship continued on its way, but did not get far. A few days later, just a few miles from its destination, the *Isaac G. Jenkins* sank in a storm. The entire crew was lost, all except the captain's dog. Somehow, despite the torrents and tumult of the angry lake, he was able to swim to shore.

DRESSED IN BLACK AND PRESENT AT FUNERALS
• THE CLERGY SHOULD REMAIN ASHORE •
PRIESTS WILL ONLY BRING BAD LUCK ON A SHIP

WHEN A WARM SOUTHERN BREEZE SUBSIDES AND A NORTHERN GALE BEGINS TO BLOW, THE DARK CLOUDS LINGERING IN THE NOVEMBER SKY WILL TUMBLE AND CHURN WITH SNOW AND ICE, AND THE ONCE CALM WATERS WILL PITCH AND HEAVE

35 FOOT WAVES • BLINDING SNOW AND SHEETS OF ICE • WINDS OF 100 MILES PER HOUR

BEWARE
► THE ◄
WITCH OF NOVEMBER

THE COLD NORTH WIND HOWLS AND THE LAKE'S ROILING WATERS CHURN, ROLLING OVER DECKS AND LAYING DOWN SHEET UPON SHEET OF HEAVY ICE, FREEZING RIGGING AND RAILING ALIKE, WHILE SHIPS ARE TOSSED, TORN, AND BROKEN ON THE CRUEL WAVES

•

MORE SHIPS HAVE SUCCUMBED TO NOVEMBER'S FURY THAN ANY OTHER MONTH OF THE YEAR

GOODBYE • DROWN • GOOD LUCK
NEITHER WHISPER NOR SPEAK NOR UTTER THESE WORDS NOT IN JEST NOR IN HEARTFELT SINCERITY
LEST YOU INVITE ILL FORTUNE TO SAIL WITH YOU

YOUR LEFT FOOT
AS WELL AS YOUR LEFT HAND ARE INCLINED TO EXICUTE THE DEVIL'S BIDDING
ALWAYS BOARD A SHIP WITH YOUR RIGHT FOOT FIRST
TO BOARD A SHIP LEFT FOOT FIRST IS TO GO STRIDE FOR STRIDE WITH SATAN!

⸙ GHOST MOOSE ⸙

MAINE · UNITED STATES

Morning's light has just begun to wake from its nocturnal slumber. A late September haze has yet to burn off, drifting in waves through aspen and larch, covering tree and underbrush in a layer of morning damp.

There amongst the fog, a massive moose saunters through the wood, as if drifting along within the ethereal brume. Glowing faintly in the dawn gloom, it stands no less than 15 feet high at its shoulders, with antlers splayed into a huge, formidable rack. Its white hide scarred from gash and gunshot, it is a ghostly revenant of a long extinct, primitive breed of moose. Long legs, bent and knobbed like trunks of birch, stretch from the ground up to its massive torso. A broken arrow juts out from its rounded hump. Impossibly large, it meanders majestically through the wood like a king surveying the vast lands of his kingdom, before stopping some 25 yards away.

Slowly lifting your bow and drawing the string back, you hold the arrow for a moment, then exhale and release. Its flight true, the arrow sails unerringly toward its mark, piercing the beast just behind the front leg. Bellowing angst, it violently lurches forward and flees into the morning mist. In pursuit, you search for any signs of blood to help with tracking the beast, but to your astonishment, none can be found. Roars and bellows echo through the wood as you track further and further through deep snow, covering terrain that seems impossible for an animal so bulky to penetrate. Occasionally glimpsing the creature in the distance, but never attaining a clear shot, you track on, mile after mile, following your prey.

Now hanging low in the western sky, the sun paints the snow in orange and yellow as trees stand shadowed against the horizon. Fog rises again, floating weightlessly from the valley below, and there in its hazy umbrage stands the white moose. Slowly drawing back a notched arrow, quietly, half out of breath, you release it. Arching high, the flight is once again true, and appears to strike the beast mid-torso, just as it dissipates into the haze.

They'll look for you tomorrow, your friends and family. They'll find your thermos – coffee half drunk and possibly still warm. They may even find your arrow embedded in the trunk of a tree. But they won't find you, at least not now . . . maybe they will try again in spring, months from now, once the winter has thawed.

THE FORTUITY OF A PORCUPINE

SPOTTING A PORCUPINE ON A HUNT BRINGS GOOD LUCK
KILLING ONE WILL BRING MISFORTUNE

HONOR
YOUR PREVIOUS HUNTS

REMOVE YOUR HAT • MAKE AN OFFERING
• PAUSE FOR A MOMENT OF REFLECTION •

TAKE A MOMENT TO HONOR THE LIFE THEY GAVE YOU
WHEN CROSSING A SPOT WHERE AN ANIMAL WAS KILLED
DURING A PREVIOUS HUNT

KILL NO OTHER ANIMAL
THAN THAT WHICH YOU ARE HUNTING

THEIR SPIRITS WILL BE CONFUSED AND LOST
THEY MAY EVEN FOLLOW YOU HOME

BE WARY
OF AN UNKINDESS OF RAVENS

THEY GIVE AWAY YOUR PRESENCE • WARN THE PREY OF THE WOOD • MAKE FOR AN UNLUCKY HUNT

YET BE WARNED!

BAD LUCK WILL FOLLOW ANYONE WHO KILLS A RAVEN

Just south of Lake Ontario, among 11 long and narrow lakes known as the Finger Lakes, live the Cayuga, also known as the Gayogohó:no? (meaning "People of the Great Swamp"). A very principled people, their way of life was an inspiration to the Founding Fathers of the United States, who adopted many governing principles from those of the Cayuga.

Living in the unforgivingly harsh environment of the north, the Cayuga have always known that the only way to survive is through cooperation and harmony. This belief was the foundation of their community, and they put rules in place to ensure its continued existence.

It isn't just the fear of punishment for breaking the rules that keeps people living together peacefully, though. The Caygua also fear the wrath of a terrifying entity known as Oniate.

In the Cayuga language, Oniate literally translates to "dry hand," but the true nature of this specter is far more sinister than this simple translation suggests. The Oniate appears as a desiccated hand, disembodied and floating in mid-air, its flesh pale and decaying, its fingers bloated and black from disease or frostbite. In some instances, the hand is still attached to its forearm, which appears to have been twisted and ripped off.

Prowling desolate and forbidden locations, Oniate ensures that no one dares to enter, or if they do, they will regret doing so for the remainder of their short lives. By simply brushing the skin of those who offend it, the Oniate can inflict blindness, or an infection that results in a prolonged and painful death, and forces its victim to watch their body slowly putrefy before their very eyes.

It isn't just those who venture into forbidden lands who suffer this fate. The Oniate can also be summoned to deal with those in the community who behave in a disagreeable or disrespectful manner. Appearing in the darkness of night, Oniate punishes those who foment discord or incite unrest within the village, those who speak ill of others – specifically the dead – and also punishes those who spread gossip or promote distrust or feuds. Once it is set upon the offending community member, Oniate pursues them every night until it inflicts its own justice – with a single touch of their skin.

NOVA SCOTIA * CANADA

The family were sat around the kitchen table – Alexander, Janet and their newly adopted teenage daughter Mary. Lunch was set and they were celebrating Mary's arrival. It was Mary who first noticed the smell of smoke, but she was shy and unfamiliar with the home, so remained silent. It was only when smoke billowed out from the adjacent room that Alexander stood and rushed to extinguish a small but growing fire. It was inexplicable – the fire seemed to have just burst into existence from nothing.

This was just the start of strange occurrences on the farm. A week after Mary's arrival, the horses were found with their tails braided together. A few days after that, the calves were found in the hay mow, gorging themselves on the recently harvested spring oats. It soon became apparent that Mary may not have traveled to the farm on her own, that perhaps a more nefarious entity had come right along with her.

More fires flared up around the farm, too – mostly insignificant, but when a tool shed exploded in a fiery ball of combustibles, Alexander called upon his neighbors. Believing an arsonist might be responsible, the group decided to keep a nightly watch in an attempt to uncover the perpetrator, but no clues, or suspects, were ever found.

The fires continued to happen, now with the accompaniment of violent knocking and slamming sounds. In one instance, wet towels burst into flame in the kitchen and the flames jumped to the larder, igniting the tallow and pork fat within. This was the final straw for Alexander, who, at his wits' end, yelled furiously into the house. He cursed the cause of all the unfortunate events, and demanded that the source show itself. In that moment, Alexander felt the great, painful slap of a phantom hand across his face. It was as if whatever was causing the trouble could sense his fear and frustration, and wanted to mock his anger. The family left the farm that very afternoon, abandoning the home and land for good.

Over the decades, the structures fell into disrepair, and fires burned most of them down completely. Only overgrown foundations, rusty nails and hinges, shingles and bricks remain. Yet, even these ruins present a danger. It is said that when items have been removed from the property, those who have taken them have, in time, seen their own homes inexplicably burned to the ground.

~<∈∃ BAYKOK ∃∋>~

GREAT LAKES REGION OF CANADA
AND THE UNITED STATES

Night has fallen in the woods. The songs of crickets and katydids rise, fall, and rise again – a reassuring sign that nothing is lurking in the darkness. Any solace from their song, however, is soon shattered when a shrill cry slices through the blackness. Forlorn yet ravenous, frantic and savage, the scream brings about an eerie silence. In the distance, a pale, gaunt shape scurries among the dark shadows of the trees, and the sound of cracking bones echoes through the stillness.

The Baykok's story reveals the enduring power of anger and resentment. During the coldest days of winter, a hunter became lost in the forest and froze to death. He rose from the dead as the Baykok – a creature full of hate toward those it saw as being responsible for its death. Refusing to leave its earthly body, the Baykok, now a corpse, roams the woods where it died, seeking revenge on anyone who crosses its path.

Emaciated and pale, the Baykok's skin is translucent, revealing its decimated inner organs. It resembles a skeleton draped in rotting skin. The Baykok only hunts in the darkness of night – its eyes, black and soulless, stare ahead – empty holes that somehow observe but cannot be discerned. Driven by its anger, the Baykok seeks out the solitary, only hunting those who travel alone; it never attacks a group.

The purest example of its ruthlessness is the manner in which the Baykok stalks its prey – silently observing them for days, learning their habits, their weaknesses and their strengths. When the Baykok finally attacks, it does so in the depth of night, creeping up while its target is sleeping deeply. Stealthily slicing open its victim's abdomen, the Baykok reaches in and savagely tears out their liver, devouring it in a ravenous frenzy. Finding a rock the same size and shape as a liver, the Baykok then fills the void created by the stolen organ, sews up its victim and uses magic to heal the wound.

The following morning, its prey awakens none the wiser, seemingly unaffected by the attack. It will be days until the effects of the replacement rock-liver are felt by the victim, but a gradual decline will ensue – including fever, lethargy and illness – as they slowly wither away.

·❧ DELTOX MARSH MONSTER ❧·

WISCONSIN * UNITED STATES

You don't have to drive too far in Wisconsin before you find yourself in the middle of nowhere.

Back in 1964, three hunters were out in the Deltox Marsh, an area along Wisconsin's Wolf River. Two of the men had broken off to drive deer toward the third, and it was while they were methodically trudging through ankle deep snow that they saw it – a powerfully built creature, lumbering through the sedge on its hind legs, standing at eight or nine feet tall, and weighing in at an estimated 600 pounds. The creature was covered in long, dark-brown hair, except for its face and hands which had a grayish-blue coloring. They watched in complete silence as the creature – seemingly unaware it was being observed – walked ahead of them, moving toward the third hunter, who had also seen the beast from a distance while sitting in his tree stand.

Word spread, and the following week the three men were joined in the marsh by a group of nine additional hunters. They spread out in a line to drive the deer ahead of them, and one after the other they each saw the creature as it passed by, about 20 feet away. This time, the creature knew the hunters were there. At times, it seemed to be watching them, toying with them, perhaps trying to gauge their mettle. As the hunters moved forward, the creature moved further out; as they backed off, it moved forward. It moved effortlessly through the snowy marsh, appearing and vanishing with ease. The creature stayed close by the entire day – a silent observer to every move the hunters made. When it was nowhere to be seen, there was an eerie quiet, save the occasional snap of a tree branch breaking. The hunters felt the unnerving, ever-present sensation of being watched.

A local parks warden later claimed to have found the place where the Wisconsin Yeti had been bedding down, describing a large area of flattened vegetation near where the hunters had their sightings. The warden believed that the creature was vegetarian, since the surrounding canary grass had been eaten down to the water line, but a deer carcass nearby had been left untouched. Most unusual of all, the warden also found a large cache of beer cans and bottles that had been drunk dry.

⟡ BANSHEE OF THE BADLANDS ⟡

SOUTH DAKOTA * UNITED STATES

Traveling westward across South Dakota, the Badlands rise from the plains like a great number of serrated knives pointing up toward the heavens; an ancient sea bottom worn by wind and weather into a labyrinth of deep canyons and sharp peaks. Desolate and unforgiving, this inhospitable terrain lacks any type of vegetation. Rattlesnakes and prairie hares make their homes here among the coyotes and wolves of the western states. Open coal seams smoke and smolder, earning this area the nickname "hell with the fires out."

During the years of the great migration west, this became the final stop for many lost or unfortunate travelers. Either due to the harsh conditions of the land itself, or through the violence of human nature, many lives have been lost to this terrain. Bandits and thieves, wild men on the run and soldiers fighting on both sides of the Battle of the Badlands regularly used the unkindness of this land to rob and murder the innocent, hiding the evidence among the spires, buttes and canyons of the Badlands. This may have been the story of the Banshee's unfortunate end, too – murdered in the wild and stowed away between rocks just south of Watch Dog Butte, never to be found again.

Lightning flashes in the sky, and glints of phosphor glimmer in its brightness. Desperate and mournful wails whip across the land along with the winds, stirring up dirt and dust. In the distance, her hair blows wildly in the wind, her limbs shake and swing in the gale. Her cries cut through the night, echoing from canyon to canyon, frightful and chilling. Distant thunder grumbles as lightning continues to blaze overhead, and the wind gusts carry her wispy form along with them. Her anguished face wrinkles in wretchedness, and wails and screams bawl from her unnaturally gaping mouth. With her arms outstretched, desperate and distraught, she hopelessly pleads, disheartened and despairing, as if demanding a reason for something unexplained, or asking a question to which there is no answer. Her tormented cries echo around for well over an hour, melancholy and forlorn, until at last she relents. Then, turning and wringing her hands, she disappears as mysteriously as she appeared.

· ALL GURGLE & NO GUTS ·

THERE'S NO ROOM FOR BRAGGARTS · DEEDS SPEAK LOUDER THAN WORDS

CODE OF THE RATTLESNAKE

NEVER SHOOT AN UNARMED MAN NOR AN UNWARNED ENEMY NOR A MAN FACING AWAY FROM YOU

ORDER NOTHING WEAKER THAN WHISKEY

ALWAYS FILL YOUR GLASS TO THE BRIM

NEVER WINCE AFTER TAKING A SHOT!

LEST YOUR GUN HAND'S ABSENCE INFERS AN UNKINDLY INTENTION

· NEVER PICK UP A DRINK · WITH YOUR RECESSIVE HAND

TAKE MEASURE OF A PERSON BY WHO THEY ARE TODAY

NEVER INQUIRE ABOUT THEIR PAST

TEND TO YOUR HORSE AHEAD OF YOURSELF

· FOOD · WATER · BED ·

·❦❧❦ HIGH HAT ❦❧❦·

NEW YORK ✳ UNITED STATES

The western edge of New York sinks toward Lake Ontario and into a heavily wooded marshland known as the Western Door. Mostly uninhabitable, the swamps are thick with vegetation and broad-rooted trees growing heavy with moss. For over a thousand years this land has been home to the Indigenous Seneca people who have shared these wilds with a sinister resident known as High Hat.

Wandering through the darkness of night, he keeps to the quiet and desolate back roads of the swamps. A tall black stovepipe hat sits atop his long head, his wiry body dressed all in black. The sight of him walking, his long strides stretching out before him, fills even the most courageous of people with an intense terror. The reek of his decaying flesh can cause temporary paralysis, or even mania. There are those who believe his presence is a sign of great misfortune to come.

Tall and lean, he has been seen standing straight-backed and strong, dark and shaded, hidden among the lofty trees. Seeking out those who have lost their way within the decay and detritus of the marshlands, he waits patiently for his opportunity to strike. His face is stark and narrow with deep-set eyes that incessantly scan the shadows of the marsh. A long, hooked nose sniffs the air, seeking even the slightest scent of a disoriented meal. Stretched over a gaping mouth full of sharp teeth, High Hat's bloodied and cracked lips pull back into an unnervingly menacing grimace. Long-fingered and broken-nailed, he fidgets in the darkness, expectantly waiting to grab and seize his prey, before wringing the life from his target's squirming body with his strong, sinewy hands. Preferring the soft young flesh of children, he often waits along the roads commonly traveled by runaway youth.

There are those who believe that High Hat is a witch, ancient and sinister – a Skudakumooch returned from the dead – as evil during his lifetime as he is now in death, and able to reanimate night after night through the sheer will of his desire to cause pain and induce fear. He becomes more powerful with each new victim he consumes. A never-ending cycle in which he is able to live each new day only through his stealing of other people's lives, one after another.

-❦❀❧ RESURRECTION MARY ❦❀❧-

ILLINOIS ✦ UNITED STATES

The night had started out lame. He was the only one of his friends who was unattached: the odd man, the spare wheel. During dinner he considered just going home. But then in the dance hall he saw her, standing on her own, leaning against the vending machine, her gorgeous, flaxen-blonde hair styled in a retro 1920s look. The sequined trim on her dress shimmered and it seemed as if she were glowing; there was a kind of a glimmer about her there in the darkness of the dance hall. He thought she was so beautiful, it took him half an hour to work up the courage to approach her.

When he finally did walk up to her, her icy-blue eyes drew him in. "Would you like to dance?" he asked, and she smiled bashfuly and nodded yes. As she offered him her gloved hand, he thought how the retro styling went beyond just her hair – even her dress and her gloves looked the part. Shy at first, she danced at arm's length from him, but as the evening wore on, they started to slow dance, her head on his shoulder. As the last song of the night played, she looked up into his eyes and they softly kissed.

Desperate to know who she was, he asked her to have a drink with him. When she said she couldn't, he asked, "Can I have your number?" She told him she didn't have one, so finally he asked, "How about I give you ride home?" She smiled timidly and accepted – he was elated! They strolled to his car hand in hand, and he even opened the passenger-side door to let her in. He asked, "Where to?" and she replied, "Head south on Archer Road, just past Bedford Park." As they drove south, he asked her a lot of questions, but still found he was doing most of the talking.

It was a cool summer night and a thin haze had developed over the road. As they drove through Bedford Park he asked, "How much further?" to which she replied, "Not far." The fog was much heavier now. "Here!" she suddenly exclaimed, and he hit the brakes and pulled the car over, near to what appeared to be a cluster of commercial buildings. Thinking she had to be joking about this being where she lived, he half-laughed and asked, "Here, yeah?" She nodded, then shimmied over in her seat, leaned in to kiss him goodnight, then silently got out of the car. To his total bewilderment, she hurried across the hazy street, directly toward the gates of Resurrection Cemetery. Once safely across the road, she turned, blew him a kiss, and, rushing through the cemetery gates, dissipated into the fog.

·─◦◦◦ SNARLY YOW ◦◦◦─·
WEST VIRGINIA ∗ UNITED STATES

The Appalachians on the eastern side of West Virginia are a vast and ancient wilderness where ridge and hollow repeat against the horizon, one after another. A land of ancient specters and restless spirits, this is a place where the long twilight shadows are not always cast by trees.

The first Europeans to arrive here were German immigrants who established the settlement of Mecklenburg. The settlers formed a good relationship with the Nahyssan people, with whom they traded supplies and animal furs, and they went to work taming the land. But, as most tales of taming the wilderness go, just as you begin to feel safe, things start to turn.

It began one blustery fall night, when the settlers heard what sounded like the howl of a wolf. A lone wolf was not much of a concern, but as time passed, the howls got nearer and became louder, and started to continue all night long. The settlers remained confident that the wolf would keep its distance, but as a precaution, they started a nightly patrol.

On one particularly dark night, a watchman heard the dull padding of paws striding over dirt. Lantern in one hand and rifle in the other, he ran in the direction of the sound, but to his bewilderment, when he got there it had stopped. Raising his lantern to brighten the darkness, all he could see were long shadows cast from nearby trees. He moved the lantern from one side to the other to see if anything was hiding in the darkness, and then he saw it. Slinking from one dark shadow to another, as lean and long as if it were a shadow itself, it appeared to have no significant shape, yet was easily discerned; it moved as fluid – viscous and black as ink. Then, just as quickly as it had appeared, it was gone, evanescing into the shadows of the nearby trees. The watchman looked around, but to no avail – whatever had been there had vanished.

A few days later, a woodsman was making his way home at twilight. With his axe over one shoulder and a lunch pail in his other hand, he was eager to get home and was taking long, quick paces. Suddenly, he froze, his wits unable to comprehend the scene before him. There in the shadows on the path ahead, a shape began to form. Rising slowly from the darkness was a hunched and bristled back. Two flaming red eyes burst from the low shadows to his left, as if the creature had been awakened abruptly from slumber, and two pointed ears and a long gaping maw were quick to materialize afterward. Night and darkness from all around coalesced, taking the shape of a massive black hound. Looking about, it seemed to the woodsman that there was nowhere that the hound was not – its tail and hindquarters stood to his side, its body stretched around behind him, and the hound's head and shoulders stood in the path before him, lips pulled back in a toothy grimace, eyes burning red as coals. A low liquid growl, guttural and gravelly, surrounded him as if the entire wood had come to life.

The woodsman dropped his pail and defiantly grasped his axe with both hands, in a move that seemed to incense the creature. It leapt toward him as he swung his axe at the beast, and although his aim was true, the blade passed through the animal as if it were made of nothing. The hound, however, found its mark, and clamped down on the woodman's throat. He felt sharp claws digging into his arm and a heavy weight on his chest, the crushing pressure of the creature gnawing at his neck, the gurgling of his blood leaving his body. And then – darkness.

The woodsman woke up on the path the following morning, and to his astonishment he was not wounded. Had he dreamt it? Had he lost his mind? Collecting himself he found his pail, and as he picked up his axe, he saw tracks in the dirt – paw prints larger than his hands, pressed into the damp path.

In the years since, the town has grown and changed its name to Shepherdstown, but sightings of the Snarly Yow continue. The creature is always standing on a path, challenging and goading travelers. Some have shot at the animal, but even bullets pass right through it. Although none of the attacks have resulted in death from the beast itself, there have been a few people who appear to have died from fright, rather than injury. So, if you plan to hike the wilds of West Virginian Appalachia, tread lightly, and be sure you've got a healthy heart.

— APPALACHIAN LORE —

WANDER NOT THESE
WOODS
PAST DARK!

DO NOT NAP OR SLUMBER WITHIN ITS TWILIGHT UMBRAGE

NEITHER
SHOUT NOR HOOT NOR HOLLER NOR CATERWAUL
NEVER WHISTLE IN THESE WOODS
LEST THE SPIRITS THAT MAY BE LISTENING
ANSWER YOUR CALL!

DO NOT FIX YOUR GAZE AIMLESSLY UPON THE TREES
AS THAT WHICH IS HIDDEN IN THE FOLIAGE
MAY FEEL AS IF YOU HAVE SEEN IT

► THESE ARE BUT A FEW OF THE RULES YOU MUST HEED IF YOU INTEND TO SURVIVE ◄
APPALACHIA!

CYCLONE ANNIE

ILLINOIS * UNITED STATES

Annie lived a few miles from the edge of town on a small plot of land between two corn fields. The old woman kept to herself, walking to town once a week for a few groceries and the occasional bottle of rye whiskey. Although she was an unassuming woman, she often attracted the attention of groups of rambunctious teens, and it was only a matter of time before talk of her unusual quietness and solitary life transitioned to name calling – "crazy," "kook" and "loon." When the farmers in the area had an outbreak of tuberculosis in their herds, a new name for old Annie began to circulate in the small community, spoken in whispers and hushed tones: "Witch."

The whispers soon became open talk and insults, and quiet accusations turned to calls for action. Soon Annie was no longer welcome at the grocery store. Dares and challenges led to hostile pranks, first in town and then at her home. Eventually, this peacable woman was forced to become aggressive, running out of her house at night waving a cane and yelling at the kids to get off her property and to leave her be.

Late one night, the townsfolk formed a mob and burned Annie's house down. As she angrily yelled about retribution, her heart gave out and she died on the spot, lying in the dirt in front of her burning home. Everything had come to its ultimate conclusion, or so the townsfolk assumed.

It was a year later to the day when lighting flashed and streaked across the black sky, and thunderclaps rumbled incessantly. What had started as a welcome August rain soon became much more violent. The winds picked up as funnel clouds formed, dropping winding tails to the ground, twisting and tearing trees from the soil and flattening crops. By morning, a massive tornado had ripped a half-mile-wide swath right through the center of the area, destroying the small town, killing 37 people, and injuring 800.

As the survivors came up out of their storm shelters, a strange scene unfolded. There, walking through the rubble and debris, was a solitary woman, old and bent, dressed head to toe in black and unknown by anyone who saw her. Yet, despite the woman's face being unfamiliar, there were those who thought they recognized the lone woman, the way she carried herself, the resolve in her stride. Though none would admit it, and many had watched her die, they knew it was Annie they saw, on her way for a few groceries and a bottle of rye.

-·⚬⊰ NA LOSA FALAYA ⊱⚬·-
SOUTHEAST UNITED STATES

Seen at first from a distance, the Na Losa Falaya is easily mistaken for a fellow traveler. It is only when a friendly wave is responded to in an eerie, almost mirrored motion, that the realization dawns that this thing, this "Long Black Being," is not human.

Making its home deep in the forest, most likely near the standing waters and stagnant decay of a swamp, the Na Losa Falaya stalks the footpaths and trails that are thought to provide safety for those traveling through the loneliest parts of the wilderness. The Na Losa Falaya watches its prey from a distance, unseen and quietly, so the unsuspecting traveler may not even realize it's there. When Na Losa Falaya first appears, it's as a dark form moving among the dense obscurities of dusk, dashing across the path ahead, dancing in and out of the shadows, melting into the darkness in one place and rising out of it in another. Sometimes it cries out from afar, mimics other people's voices, weeps, or calls for help.

It's only when the Na Losa Falaya makes its presence known that its true appearance is revealed: a long-shriveled face, narrow, squinting eyes – as black as the skin surrounding them, and discernable only by their glossiness – long pointed ears and long dark hair, damp and clinging. Those unfortunate enough to look upon the Long Black Being are so unsettled that they immediately lose consciousness.

This is the moment when the Na Losa Falaya strikes, not with rage or ferocity, but with a simple prick of a locust thorn. When they awaken, the victim has no idea what has occurred, and is totally unaware of the spell that has been placed on them. In time, a subtle irritability will set in. The victim's new, surly disposition will steadily intensify, until loud outbursts and mean words become anger and physical rage. An insidious fury eventually arises, compelling the victim to murder those closest to them.

Some say that you will recognize the Na Losa Falaya because it hovers slightly above the ground. Others have seen Long Black Beings slither along the edges of paths and trails like snakes – just waiting for a traveler to make even the slightest of wrong steps. Either way, when you walk in the wilderness, keep your wits about you.

-ॐ THE BOY WITH THE CROOKED SMILE ॐ-
BAJA * MEXICO

For most of us, kindness is in our nature; when we see someone in need, we offer what we can to help them. Whether out of callousness, excessive exposure or simply feeling taken advantage of, as the years pass, we sometimes become less willing to help. And sometimes, we might feel like there are so many people in need, we don't even know where to begin.

The sun had set and the dusty street was poorly illuminated. Shadows were cast all along the path ahead, so when a small boy stepped out from the darkness, head down and hand raised, he gave the young doctor quite a fright. "*Por favor, señor, please, veinte centavos, diez, cinco centavos ...* anything, sir," he begged. Surprised, the flustered man reached into his pocket and retrieved a handful of coins and gave them to the child. The boy slowly raised his face to the young doctor and smiled. It was a ghastly smile that revealed crooked teeth in crimsoned gums, angular and jagged, that emerged from behind bloodied and torn lips. "*Muchas gracias señor*, much thanks," said the boy. His black eyes turned up at the corners as he pocketed the coins and ran off. The doctor hurried home and, believing he had just seen a demon or spirit, locked his door before a fitful night's sleep.

Several nights later, a police sergeant, an older man, was walking to meet his friends at *la taberna* when out of the shadows the small boy appeared again. Once more with his hands raised and head down he asked, "*Por favor, señor, please, veinte centa . . .*" "GET OUTTA HERE!" the officer shouted, pushing the boy out of his path and to the ground without halting his stride. As he glanced back toward the boy, he saw him standing in the shadow of large tree, his white teeth, visibly mangled, crooked and sharp, glowing in the darkness. Hands on his hips, the boy let out a malicious and sinister cackle before slowly pointing at the policeman, then running off into the darkness.

The officer thought it a bit odd, but felt no remorse for his rough treatment of the child and continued on his way.

The following day, the police officer was found dead in his home having suffered a massive cardiac event. Even after all his years of service to the community, his heart simply hadn't been big enough.

~❧ LA MALOGRA ❧~

SOUTHWESTERN UNITED STATES
AND NORTHERN MEXICO

In spring, the cottonwood trees drop their seeds, enrobed in the airy white fluff that gives them their name. On a windy day, these seeds can travel as far as 20 miles before they find a place to rest. Slightly sticky and light as a feather, the fluff clings to branches and covers the ground in a blanket of white. If the seeds can't find a footing, the fluff binds up in loose bundles and comes to life in the breeze, scurrying across the ground and dancing in swirling gusts, finally coming to rest in quiet corners, culverts and anyplace away from the grasp of spring winds. It's within these dark spaces that La Malogra finds its way.

A truly malicious entity, La Malogra enters a small bundle of fluff as it begins to form, then immediately seeks more. As it joins another bundle, and then another, it methodically becomes a massive ball of fluff, ever moving, never still; shifting with the wind, without shape, yet entirely tangible. In appearance, it looks as if La Malogra is as light as the air that carries it, but in reality, it is crushingly heavy. It expands and contracts, undulating unpredictably, striking out in an instant and pulling back in the next. Its movements appear arbitrary, yet La Malogra maneuvers with calculated accuracy. The mere sight of this incomprehensible being has driven some to madness instantly, while those who have had the good fortune to maintain their sanity while witnessing these malevolent and wild undulations have been found the following day, frozen in fright. La Malogra is a terrible misfortune, stalking the forests and countryside, hunting for those who, not unlike itself, seek darkness – those who are intent on behaving badly.

La Malogra wastes no time when it crosses the path of its prey, moving quickly to engulf its target, picking them off the ground and causing instant disorientation, constricting and squeezing until the breath is pulled out of them. The following morning, the victim is found asphyxiated – their lungs, nose and mouth full of cottonwood seed, their body covered in a blanket of white fluff, as if tucked in for a long, cold night's sleep.

··❀ CHINDI ❀··
SOUTHWESTERN UNITED STATES

When we imagine the spirits of the dead, we often see them as they were in life – capable of a full spectrum of traits and emotions. Those who perished in a horrific fashion might be holding on to their last gruesome thoughts, but we still see them as well-rounded and whole in their emotional abilities. Imagine, then, if a spirit were to manifest itself with only the extremely negative traits of its human self – anger, hate, fear, jealousy and aggression – and all the sins of its human life, everything bad and unbalanced. This is the way of the Chindi – the spirit that escapes its mortal bond through a person's dying breath, according to traditional Navajo belief.

Once the Chindi is released, it seeks out people and possessions that it knew well in life, but simply being near the negative energy of a Chindi can cause serious harm to the living. The Navajo call this "ghost sickness," and its relentless presence and negative energy manifests in living humans as small mishaps – misfortunes that at first might be overlooked, but which over time can result in fatigue, fever, nausea, listlessness, hallucinations and eventually death. For this reason, the possessions of the deceased are oftentimes destroyed, and their name is never spoken again, for fear of attracting the Chindi. In an ideal situation, death occurs outdoors, allowing the dying's final breath to disperse on the winds. If someone dies in their home, however, those who remain have little choice but to abandon the building, knowing the Chindi now resides there.

Some choose to use the Chindi for their own evil pursuits. Shaman can summon a Chindi by digging up a piece of its corpse. Through dark magic, they can bind the Chindi to someone of their choosing, with the intent of causing harm; by grinding up a piece of the corpse's bone into a fine powder, and mixing it into food, a shaman can poison someone with ghost sickness.

Once a Chindi has bound itself to someone, there is very little that can be done. Even moving from one place to another, attempting to hide oneself through constant relocation, will have little effect – the Chindi is always there, wielding its negativity to cause constant strife. The Chindi's lurking presence, just a step behind, is forever sowing discontent, bending will, and in the end, breaking it.

CRYBABY MONSTER

NEW MEXICO * UNITED STATES

It was a cool October night, back in 1966, when static cut through the evening radio programming in Albuquerque's South Valley. There had been quite a bit of this over the past few weeks, but on this night, there was more static than programming. After a few whacks, and an antenna adjustment or two to no avail, most folks turned off their radios, settling in to enjoy a crisp autumn evening instead. That's when they heard it – distant at first, then nearer and louder – the sound of a crying baby. Some people came out of their homes to search, thinking there was an infant in distress.

The first person to see the source of the sound described it as a black shape, a hole cut in the darkness of night. It looked like someone crouching close to the ground, facing the opposite direction. Thinking it might be a neighbor, the concerned citizen called out to see who it was, but when the creature stood and turned to face them, they knew instantly it was like nothing they had seen before. It was the shape of a man, about five feet tall, entirely black except for its face, which was completely white and featureless.

The citizen yelled again, and the creature turned and ran off on all fours, more like an animal than a man. Its escape took it in the direction of a father and his 18-year-old son who were also looking for the crying baby. In a hurried fury, the creature hit the son hard in the chest, knocking him to the ground before running off into the dark.

Over the next few nights, the creature was seen lurking as far north as Old Town Bridge. Although it wasn't seen again in South Valley, it was heard almost nightly for nearly a full month, the sound being described as "the most horrible cry, like a baby." Not only did radios continue to cut out, some also said that while the creature was around, cats wouldn't meow, and dogs would cower behind furniture, refusing to move. The young man who was struck by the creature claimed that anytime it was near, his chest would throb with pain. One resident recalled a similar creature making the rounds back in the forties, wondering out loud, "How does it cry without a face?"

⊸❦⊱ GRAY MAN ⊰❦⊸
SOUTH CAROLINA ✶ UNITED STATES

The weather seems fair as large cumulus clouds hang heavy in the distant sky, meandering sluggishly across the hazy horizon like a herd of white elephants crossing the savanna. A strong breeze rushes over the cresting surf, carrying with it the salty taste of sea spray, tousling dampened hair and pulling at loose clothing. Ten-foot swells march one after another to shore, the rhythmic whoosh and roar of strong waves pushing pebbles and debris inland. Over the lifeguard's hut a yellow flag flutters in the wind, warning of the hazardous surf.

The day must have been much like this one when, on September 23, 1822, he mounted his horse and rode out from Georgetown toward Pawleys Island. He was on his way to see his fiancée for a visit, and while there, he was hoping to convince her and her family to move further inland for safety, in the face of an imminent incoming storm. Although he'd been riding hard, he was behind time. With the sun falling quickly in the sky behind him, he decided to take a shortcut through the salt marshes just between the mainland and Pawleys Island.

The gray hues of twilight were upon him as he broke from the road and entered the tall grasses of the marsh. Throughout the day, the ocean swells had grown and made their way further inland, and by the time he began to make his way through the thick spartina and mud, the soil had been fully saturated, turning the marsh's earth into loose, unsupportive muck. It wasn't long before his horse was mired down in the soft ground. Struggling to free itself only made things worse, and as the mud continued to give way, both steed and rider were pulled down under the salty soil and drowned.

Eagerly awaiting his arrival, the young man's fiancée spent the night unable to sleep. She rose early the next morning and raced downstairs, fully expecting to find him waiting for her in the parlor, but to her disappointment, he wasn't there. She checked to see if he'd sent word ahead of his departure, however, much to her concern, she was told none had come. She went to the stables to inquire about his arrival, but she was met with no news of his whereabouts. Her anxiety began to rise.

She went to the shore along a path they often walked together, trying to calm herself with the familiar sound of the rising surf. It was mid-morning, and by now the sky was overcast, the heavy clouds of the evening had been driven off by thinner cirrus clouds which raced across the sky. The breeze, no longer gentle, had grown to gusts, as a full wind rustled through the creaking boughs, brushing wisps of loose hair across her furrowed brow.

The young woman became more and more concerned about her fiancé; he had never been this late and he'd never be so irresponsible as to travel when a storm was incoming. Her mind raced from one horrible misfortune to another as the surf became wilder. She wandered further down shore, watching the sea foam as it swirled over the surface of the water, when there in distance she saw him, standing in the gray haze and sea spray of the imminent storm. It had to be him, a man with the same stature and form as her own true love. She ran to him, but as she made her way closer, although she recognized his face, she was struck with dismay by its countenance. His eyes, somber and apprehensive were full of sadness and foretold of the tempest to come. Although he spoke not a single word as he took both her hands in his, when his eyes fixed on hers she saw the journey where he had meant his fate, witnessed the moment he met his end – she felt the extent of his adoration for her and the infinite sadness of his final moments, the concern he had for her and her family's safety. His eyes, all filled with a sense of sorrowful presentiment told her this and more, until in a gust of wind, he vanished leaving her, in solitude ahead of the approaching gale..

Heartbroken and full of grief, she ran home and told her family about what had just occurred. She conveyed to them the sense of foreboding, the intensity of the message her lost love had tried to give them. Heeding the warning, the family gathered their pets and the few possessions they could carry and headed inland for safety ahead of the storm.

And what a storm it was. On September 27, 1822, hundreds died when a storm surge rapidly flooded low-lying areas. Homes were washed away, and entire families were lost to the sea.

To this day, the Gray Man walks the shore of Pawleys Island ahead of destructive storms. Name a hurricane, and there will be those who claim to have seen him before it hit. He was there before Hazel in 1954, then again in 1989 before Hugo's devastating landfall, and he was there once more before Florence in 2018. Strolling the lonely shore in his long gray coat, he is a sinister revenant of a life forfeited and a love lost all those years ago.

AN EVER-POWERFUL ALLIUM

CARRY A RED ONION IN YOUR POCKET TO ENSURE YOU'LL SURVIVE ANY HORRIFIC TORRENT

BEWARE

THE SUDDEN FLIGHT OF DOGS AND CATS

UNFETTERED OR UNATTENDED DOGS AND CATS AS WELL AS OTHER SMALL PETS WILL ATTEMPT TO FLEE FOR HIGHER GROUND, SEEKING SAFETY FURTHER INLAND. IF KEPT INDOORS, THEY'LL FIDGET AND FUSS, AND NO AMOUNT OF CONSOLING WILL CALM THEIR RESTLESSNESS.

HURACAN

THE MAYAN GOD OF WIND • STORM • LIGHTNING • FIRE

FLOODED THE WHOLE WORLD AND RODE UPON THE WINDY MISTS
TO ENSURE THE TOTAL DESTRUCTION OF ALL LIFE ON THE PLANET
ONLY THEN DID HE COMMAND THE EARTH TO RISE FROM THE
DEPTHS OF THE SEA ONCE MORE, TO CREATE NEW LIFE

*

BE WARY OF
THE COLOR RED DURING THE GALE

AGGRESSIVE • VIBRANT • HOT • PASSIONATE

THE COLOR RED IS KNOWN TO ATTRACT THE FURIOUS POWER AND DESTRUCTION OF LIGHTNING

⸙ GHOST OF DEER ISLAND ⸙

MISSISSIPPI * UNITED STATES

Deer Island is the closest barrier island on the Mississippi coast, less than a quarter of a mile out from Biloxi. As a coastal reserve, it's home to a handful of endangered species, as well as being a stopping point for many migratory birds on their way south. The wild salt marshes are crowded with tall grasses, and alligators bask in the hot afternoon sun, a reminder of a more ancient time. As the island is so close to the mainland, it's also a common spot for sport fisherman trolling Biloxi Bay and beyond. But long before civilization had found its way to the southern shores of the United States, this marshy island served a more menacing purpose as a hidden treasury for pirates' plunder.

The daylight had faded faster than the two men had expected, and they found themselves packing up from a full day of fishing as the sun began to set. Although only a mile or so back to shore, the thought of crossing the bay in darkness, then unpacking and stowing their equipment on the other side was not as enticing as spending a night on the sandy beaches of Deer Island, drinking a beer or two as they ate the day's catch and told tall tales of the ones that got away. They built a fire from dry driftwood, and set about making camp and cleaning up a mix of redfish and flounder. The indigo horizon gave way to star-filled blackness, and the lights of Biloxi glimmered in the distance, reflected in the inky dark waters of the bay. The night was warm, and a soft breeze made its way in over the gulf, deterring the descent of mosquitos and their bothersome kind. The two men bedded down to the pop and snap of a waning fire. The island was quiet as the tide gently lapped the sand beach, lulling them to slumber.

Yet sleep did not come easily for the two fishermen – restless and fitful, they woke often to the sounds of wildlife. Twigs snapped and small feet scurried through the nearby brush, and larger animals also made themselves known while stalking smaller prey off in the marsh. Eventually, at around two in the morning, the men decided to stoke up the fire, crack open a few more beers and wait out the night before heading for home at daybreak. Time tends to pass slowly through the dark, unfamiliar hours of early morning – hours which most humans safely spend in slumber.

The company of a good friend lightens the mood in even the most stressful situations, and at first simply being awake and laughing at old jokes together seemed to put the uneasiness of the night to rest. The small critters were easy to ignore as they scurried about, dashing in and out of the campfire light, stealing scraps of dropped food. Even some of the louder, bigger animals didn't bother the fishermen – it was only when they heard what sounded like human feet running that they became concerned.

One grabbing a machete and the other a fillet knife, they ventured side by side into the darkness of the undergrowth. Within five feet, the ground began to give way under their steps – damp tangles of roots and decaying grass grabbed at them, seizing their feet as they continued forward. Ten feet in they were up to their knees, slogging through brackish marshland until they found themselves both laughing and shaking their heads, having found nothing. They soon agreed that their fears were just an uneasy preoccupation with the unknown sounds of the island.

As they turned to head back to camp, there, standing between them and their escape route, was the corpse of a headless man brandishing a rusty cutlass. A tattered and stained white blouse hung loosely over the fleshless ribcage. Skin clung in torn strips from his arms, and boney knees jutted out from below his leather breeches; his skinless legs and feet were muddy and intertwined with paspalum root and glasswort.

Instinctively, the men split up, one running to the left and the other to the right, which seemed to freeze the acephalous phantom in a moment of indecision. A moment was all they needed though, and they dashed past the dithering wraith and raced toward their skiff. Leaving everything behind, they pushed off into the darkness of the bay and headed for the lights of the mainland with the specter in pursuit, waving his blade as he waded waist-deep into the surf. Looking back from a safe distance, they saw the headless skeleton standing guard – a silhouette against their still-burning fire – a headless sentry to a vast, unknown treasure.

SPIT INTO THE FOAMY SWELLS BEFORE YOU SAIL
ADVANTAGEOUS CURRENTS AND THE BLESSING OF THE TIDES WILL FOLLOW

TOSS A COIN INTO THE SEA
A SMALL TOLL FOR A BIT OF PEACE OF MIND AND A SAFE VOYAGE ON NEPTUNE'S WATERS

YET TAKE HEED
CAST NO STONE UPON THE BRINY SEA AS YOU SET TO SAIL
LEST AS THE STONE DOES SINK INTO THE MURKY DEPTHS OF THE UNFORGIVING SEA
SO TOO SHALL YOUR SHIP BEFORE YOU MAKE LAND

NEVER CHANGE THE NAME OF A SHIP
YOU TEMPT THE WRATH OF NEPTUNE'S FURY • UNREGISTERED IN HIS LEDGER OF THE DEEP
YOUR SHIP WILL BE BELEAGUERED BY MISFORTUNE
HEAVING ON SWELLS • ROLLING ATOP THE DRIVING WAVES • YAWING WITH THE INCESSANT BILLOWS
UNTIL BROKEN UPON THE TIDE & PLUNGED TO THE DEPTHS OF THE BRINY DEEP

• N E I T H E R   K I L L   N O R   H A R M •
THE FEATHERED WING
OF A SWALLOW • GULL OR ALBATROSS

►THEY CARRY THE SOULS OF DEAD SAILORS◄
YOUR LUCK WILL TURN SOUR EVEN IF YOUR INTENT IS NOT MALICIOUS

A SHIP IS A TEMPERAMENTAL KIND OF VESSEL
NEVER NAME A SHIP IN HONOR OF A BETROTHED WOMAN
INCLINED TO BECOME JEALOUS OF SUCH ACTIONS
IT MAY SPITEFULLY ACT TO CAUSE HARM

···ᏚᏃᎷᎡᎡᏃᏃᏃᏃ ALTON BRIDGE GOATMAN ᏚᏃᎷᎡ···

TEXAS * UNITED STATES

The soft gurgle of water slowly passing beneath the bridge mingles with the buzzing of insects. The sun dips low, casting amber hues through the humid air. The old oxidized iron bridge offers a silhouette against the fleeting day, and its weathered wooden deck groans now and again, giving way slightly under foot. Were this not the Old Alton Bridge, the serene scene would calm your senses, but here in northeastern Texas, you wait in anxious anticipation as shadows press the amber light westward. As you summon the beast by giving three sharp knocks on a cold iron truss, the darkness seeps in, and you know you won't have to wait long.

A stone is thrown, landing in the middle of the bridge before skidding off the edge and splashing into the water below. Then another and another – an unseen assailant keeps launching stones that rain down over the wooden deck and into the creek. You take refuge at one side of the bridge – standing, waiting, as loud bellowing begins to echo through the valley. The brush rustles as low branches sway and snap and heavy feet stomp through the darkness of the undergrowth. All is quiet for a moment, until you hear the distinct sound of hard hooves clunking across the bridge.

Ca-clunk, ca-clunk . . . you slowly lift your torch, and there before you stands a frightful beast, nearly eight feet tall. Two yellow eyes stare at you, deep set in the massive head of a goat, which is crowned with large, curled horns and a mass of black, tangled, coarse hair. Its chest and arms are that of a man, but they sit atop the hindquarters of a large goat with massive cloven hooves. The creature gives a heavy snort and raises its head, emitting a forlorn bellow before once again fixing its eyes on you. Suddenly, the animal is charging toward you! Stumbling backward, you run to your car and quickly speed off, only half sure about what you've just seen, and hoping you've outrun this awful monstrosity.

ᏚᏃᎷᎡ···ᏚᏃᎷᎡᏃ

This tale is an old one, the horror of a massive half-man half-beast summoned by the simple act of three hard knocks on the cold iron of an old bridge. But when we look into the origin of this tale, the story that forms the foundation of this legend, we're faced with the age-old question of what horror truly is. We're asked to dig deep within ourselves

to find where it actually resides, and for many of us the answer is a very uncomfortable one. Recognizing that terror lives in our natural biases, which we may spend our lifetime trying to outrun. When we examine the origin of this tale we must ask ourselves what's more frightening, the monster or those small hateful men who made him.

As a hardworking goatherder, Oscar Washburn provided a good service, and quickly made a name for himself due to his quality cheese, milk and meat. It will come as no surprise, then, that as an African-American man, Oscar's success also garnered the attention of the local KKK members. Many of these hateful men held positions in local government, and as Oscar found more success, they began scheming ways to get rid of him. They didn't mind the business so much, they simply found Oscar to be a little "too . . ." Specifically, "too" successful, "too" hardworking, and worst of all, "too" well-liked by the rest of the community. So, when he became "too" bold and hung a handmade sign reading, "This way to the Goatman" on Old Alton Bridge, the city commissioner, a Klansman, ordered the county Sherriff, also a Klansman, to arrest Oscar for illegal solicitation on public property.

The Sherriff didn't exactly follow the due process of the law, though. Instead, he and a handful of other Klansmen assembled an angry and detestable mob, and with cloth flour bags pulled over their heads, they crossed the bridge and pulled Oscar from his home. They dragged him through the night, punching and kicking him all the way, laughing and joking at his expense until they made it to Old Alton Bridge. Oscar was already in a poor condition when they placed a noose around his neck and pushed him over the side of the bridge.

To the Klan's surprise, there was no sharp snap of the rope, no crack of the neck, nor choking breaths of a dying man to cheer as they had expected. As they looked over the bridge railing, they saw the rope and observed the noose, but Oscar had vanished. Scurrying down the bank, they searched the water and scoured the creek's shores, but there was no sign of the man they had tried to lynch, and Oscar Washburn was never seen again.

It is said that of all who knock on Old Alton Bridge to summon the Goatman, he only takes those with the blood of Klansmen flowing through their veins.

WESTERN LORE

WHEN UNSURE OF WHERE TO PUT YOUR HAT
BEST TO KEEP IT ON YOUR HEAD

ONLY REMOVE YOUR HAT
TO ENTER A HOME • TO MEET A LADY • OR WHILE A COFFIN PASSES BY
• THEN PLACE IT RIGHT BACK ON YOUR HEAD WHERE IT BELONGS •

A HAT ON THE BED
WILL START AN ARGUMENT • CAN BRING MISFORTUNE • A SIGN OF IMMINENT HARM
IS AN OMEN OF IMPENDING DEATH

TAKE CARE
NEVER USE THE SAME IRON ON A HORSE TWICE • IT BRINGS BAD LUCK TO THE HORSE AND ITS RIDER

NEITHER KINDNESS NOR OBLIGATION SHOULD IMPEL A GENTLEMAN TO LEND ANOTHER MAN HIS
• HAT • HORSE • GUN • BOOTS •

MIND THE NUMBER OF WHITE FEET ON A HORSE
ONE FOOT BUY HIM • TWO FEET TRY HIM • THREE FEET LEAVE HIM ALONE
FOUR FEET MAY AS WELL JUST GO ON HOME

NEVER WEAR A PAIR OF SECONDHAND BOOTS
THEY CARRY THE LUCK OF THE PREVIOUS OWNER.
GOOD OR BAD • BLESSED OR TROUBLED
THEIR FORTUNE WILL BECOME YOURS ONCE WORN

NEVER EAT CHICKEN BEFORE A FIGHT
• YOU ARE WHAT YOU EAT •

⋯⋰⋰ HAINT ⋰⋰⋯

GULLAH GEECHEE COAST * UNITED STATES

Whether we know it or not, most of us have experienced the presence of a ghost or two in our lives. An odd shiver, an inexplicable chill that raises hair and induces goosebumps on bare skin. The subtle scent of vetiver and hyacinth – a warm redolence of your deceased grandmother's vanity. The scent of your father's pipe and the distant creak of the living room floor when you know you're alone in the house. These are, perhaps, the souls of loved ones, returning now and again to check in on us, or simply watching over us in our daily pursuits.

Other ghosts include the ambient spirits of a place – those who roam the locations where they felt most comfortable during their living years. These beings are sometimes inquisitive about our living earthly existence, and can be possessive over the physical things they've lost, but they tend to mean us no harm.

None of this is the case with a Haint, however. Haints are the souls of people who lived their lives in discontent – miserable individuals who relished in the unkindness of misdeeds and petty offences, who in life used words and actions as weapons. Practitioners of deceit, these folks delighted in nothing more than gaining leverage over those around them, including family, coworkers and neighbors. Living only for their own gain, these people were often incapable of trusting anyone, were fearful and angry, and believed that everyone was out to take what was theirs.

In death, a Haint finds that moving on is intolerable and unjust. It is not only bound to its location and moored to the possessions it accumulated during life, it is also aggressively defensive of these things. Every item taken from a Haint's former home is an assault on the life it lived, every change or renovation to its former house is an afront to its presence.

A Haint envies every breath of air taken in its old dwelling, and resents every second of peace that is found by those living in its presence. It cowers in the corners of rooms, like an unbearable darkness, covetously scowling over the living. The Haint's resentment is an infestation of heaviness, a weight that presses down on the living with a slow and methodically debilitating hatred. Slow to move yet quick to anger, the Haint is ever present yet never seen, and causes an ambient aggression to seep into every fiber and grain of the place where it lingers.

It's during the darkness of night that the maliciousness of the Haint rises to untenable levels. Sleeplessly, it stalks and haunts the living as they slumber, often sitting on their chests once they're comfortably in bed. The Haint's heaviness renders even the most vibrant of us to somnolence, yet in a Haint's presence your rest will be fitful; sleep will feel within reach, but will rarely come. When it does come, it too is heavy and fraught with darkness – dreams are frustratingly confusing and often frightful. You'll find yourself waking out of a deep sleep as the Haint pokes your ribs or pulls your nose hairs. You will be confused and uncertain, or even sweating in fright.

Your nights will come to seem longer than your days, but once daylight comes, your body will ache from lack of sleep, and the frustration of sleepless nights will slowly strip you of your ability to function during the day. You'll become easily frantic and more prone to making mistakes. Friends will start to distance themselves from you, fewer people will seek out your company, and in your agitated state, the solitude will seem like a welcome respite.

Through schemes and ploys, and with hateful ambition, the Haint works slowly and methodically over time, until it successfully adds you to its list of possessions. Over days and weeks, it has made you its own, and your energy feeds it. The Haint has made the comfortable uncomfortable, the confident uncertain and the trusting suspicious. It has made you in your life as it was in its own.

HOW TO RID ONESELF OF A HAINT

PAINT YOUR PORCH CEILING BLUE
HAINTS CAN CROSS WATER — THE BLUE CEILING WILL CONFUSE THEM

*

CLEAN THE HOME
TOP TO BOTTOM, SPIC AND SPAN — USE PINE AND CAMPHOR TO MOP THE FLOORS

*

BURN SAGE
MAKE SURE TO PUSH THE SMOKE INTO THE CORNERS OF THE ROOM
LEAVE NO ROOM UNDONE

*

BUILD A BOTTLE TREE
A BOTTLE TREE WILL ENSNARE THE WANDERING SOULS — TRAPPED AND CONFUSED
THE MORNING SUN WILL DESTROY THEM

*

TOSS SALT ACROSS YOUR THRESHOLD
A HAINT CAN'T PASS BY WITHOUT COUNTING EVERY LAST GRAIN OF SALT
WHEN THEY LOSE COUNT THEIR FRUSTRATION WILL GROW. AS COCKCROW APPROACHES
THE HAINT WILL BE FORCED TO LEAVE OR BURN UP IN THE MORNING SUN

*

HANG A MIRROR
HAINTS ARE NOTORIOUSLY VAIN — A MIRROR HUNG BY THE ENTRY WILL STOP THEM IN
THEIR TRACKS AS THEY GAZE AT THEIR OWN REFLECTION

*

PASTE THE WALLS WITH NEWSPAPER
COMPELLED TO READ ALL THE ARTICLES WORD FOR WORD, THE HAINT WILL LINGER FOR
SUCH A LONG TIME THERE WILL BE NONE LEFT FOR MISCHIEF-MAKING

*

Many people have things that they like to keep to themselves – harmless secrets or interests they think others might find foolish or unusual. But there is nothing harmless about the secrets a Stikini keeps. In the light of day, a Stikini looks like a normal person, going about their life as any other. They sometimes exhibit strange behavior or difficult personalities, but it is their inability to recognize when they've flouted social norms that truly sets a Stikini apart.

A Stikini is a witch who dabbled too much at the edges of dark magic, and, over time, strayed too far into the darkness. It's in this darkness that a Stikini builds its strength. With every sinister deed, the darkness grants it more power, but it's only when the darkness bestows its most powerful gift – shapeshifting – that the true nature of a Stikini's wickedness is realized.

Once the Stikini gains the ability to shapeshift, it can transform into a misshapen and revolting half-owl, half-human enormity. Some simply appear as huge owls, but others are grotesque in their appearance, heinously aberrant – with an extra arm, or a human face – as if they hadn't fully mastered the transformation. No matter their shape, all have the ability to tear a village of grown men to pieces, and a bloodthirst capable of devouring them all.

As with all things gifted by darkness, this power does not come without a cost. To transform, the Stikini must travel deep into the woods at night, where it regurgitates its internal organs, hanging them high in a tree to keep other animals from eating them. It then falls into a fit of cracking bones, wings and beaks tearing through human skin, and talons emerging from its now-changed feet. Once reshaped, the Stikini spreads its wings and flies into the night in search of a victim. Sometimes this is a person who has offended them, other times, the choice might come down to simple convenience, but once the Stikini sets upon its prey, there is nothing that can stop them. Sitting on its target's chest, its talons ripping at flesh, the Stikini tears the victim's beating heart out through their mouth and devours it on the spot.

After its feed, the Stikini returns to its hanging organs, consumes them, and returns to human form . . . until the next time it feels bloodthirsty.

BEWARE THE LONELY HOOT OF THE OWL
A SOMBER CRY • AN OMINOUS GROWL • FIENDISH AND RASPING MOAN
• AN OMEN OF DEATH TO COME •

HOW TO KILL A STIKINI
•

FIND THEIR ORGANS HIDDEN HIGH IN A TREE • CLIMB THE HEIGHTS TO RETRIEVE THEM • TOSS THEM TO THE GROUND •

DESTROY THEM IN THE HIGH, HOT FLAME OF A FIRE

WITH THEIR INNARDS DESTROYED AND UNABLE TO TRANSFORM BACK INTO THEIR HUMAN FORM, THE STIKINI WILL BURN IN THE SUNLIGHT OF THE NEW DAY

• OR •

FASHION AN ARROW WITH A PINE SHAFT

DRESS IT WITH THE FEATHERS OF AN OWL

YOUR AIM TRUE AND YOUR MIND PURE

YOU MUST PIERCE THE HEART TO

DEFEAT THIS BEAST

•

-꿎 ROUX-GA-ROUX 꿎-

LOUISIANA * UNITED STATES

It'd been more than two weeks since anyone had seen Ol' Thibodeaux. It's true that he was a bit of a hermit, living all on his own at the far edge of the swamp, but you could always count on him for Sunday mass, and now he'd missed two in a row. His small shack, out among the moss-covered cypress trees, was held together with rusted nails and jasmine vines. The roof, heavy with lichen, grew a garden of spider lilies and irises. By the time he'd skipped his third mass, the townsfolk had also noticed that some of their livestock had gone missing, with nothing remaining but a few trails scattered with blood leading back to the swamp.

Ol' Thibodeaux missed a fourth week of mass and more animals disappeared, so a small group of men decided it was time to go and check on the hermit. By the time they arrived, the sun was high in the sky and had burned through the thick mist of the swamp air. Sure enough, the old man was home, sitting in a crooked rocking chair and chewing tobacco, covered in dried mud from his thighs down to his bare feet. His hair was a thatch of tangled strands, matted and congealed with a viscous black substance. His old hound was lying lethargically in the front yard, chained to a stake. The dog appeared not to have been fed in weeks, his ribs visible and his spine jutting from his back.

Chicken carcasses lay strewn about the yard, torn open and bloodied, covered in maggots. The air was filled with the scent of death, and flies swarmed over the arid ground. As the men approached the porch, Ol' Thibodeaux reached for his shotgun, stood up and fired a round into the air. Then he brought the barrel of the gun back down and pointed it at the men. "Y'all get now!" he yelled as the men stumbled back toward the road. One of the men tripped over the chain that bound the starving hound, pulling up the stake that tethered him, and the dog tore off down the road, dragging the chain and the stake behind him as if running for his life.

That night, what had so far just been a simple case of animals going missing took a turn for the worse and carnage spread throughout the parish. Pets and livestock alike were torn to pieces and strewn over the ground. Gators feasted on the bits of flesh and bone in the swamp. One of the men who had been out at Ol' Thibodeaux's place the day before now lay dead on his front steps, his shredded clothing bloodied and covered in muck. His chest was now a great gaping cavity, splayed open, and his organs were gone. Across his face was the frozen expression of horror experienced at the moment of his death. This could only be the work of a Roux-Ga-Roux.

The following night, the townsfolk set a trap. If this was truly a Roux-Ga-Roux, they knew that now that it had tasted human flesh, it would only want more. To end the murerous rampages, they would have to trap and kill it. On the top step of the front porch of every house in town they placed a line of thirteen shiny new pennies. Some of the townspeople set up their roofs with shotguns, others grabbed gardening tools, pitchforks and machetes while waiting for the beast to return. A full moon crawled its way up over the trees, glowing softly through the fog drifting in over the swamp. Chickens crying in the distance woke those who had dozed off and raised the hair on the necks of those who hadn't.

There in the mist, hunched and crooked, stood the beast. If it had been standing up straight it'd have easily been seven feet tall. With thick legs, bare feet and broad shoulders, it wore the tattered shirt and overalls of a much smaller human. Its hands were strong and wide, and covered in coarse black hair, each thick finger ending in a sharp black, broken nail. A massive wolf head, with a long, gaping muzzle full of sharp teeth, and eyes that glowed yellow glared out into the darkness. It slinked through the night toward one of the homes, and as it climbed the stairs, it stopped at the line of pennies across the top stair. Incapable of counting past twelve, the thirteenth penny confounded the beast, and so with utter confusion it counted from one side to the other, arriving at the extra coin only to start counting back again. Over and over it examined the pennies until a shot rang out through the night air. The creature howled into the dark as the shot grazed its left leg, and turning with a jerk, it limped off into the night.

The next visit the townsfolk would make to Ol' Thibodeaux would be with lit torches, shotguns and knives. The mist had yet to lift as they trudged toward the hermit's cabin. When they arrived, they set the ramshackle structure ablaze, and waited for its inhabitant to run out into the hands of the mob. However, when Ol' Thibodeaux finally did rush from his home, he burst through the burning wall, on fire himself from the waist up. The townspeople stood, mouths open, as the old man, his leg bandaged from the previous night's gunshot wound, sprinted across the yard toward the swamp. He dove into the murky depths of the water, never to be seen again. Every once in a while, even to this day, some of the parishes around the swamp still report unexplained deaths of livestock, and sometimes, even the disappearance of a misbehaving youth.

LOUP GAROU

IN FRENCH MEANS WEREWOLF

A GOOD PERSON WHO BECOMES A BAD CHRISTIAN WILL BE CURSED TO WANDER THE CANADIAN WILDS IN THE FORM OF A LARGE BLACK WOLF

101 DAYS AND NIGHTS THEY MUST WANDER AS A WOLF!

➤ FOR AS MINOR A SIN AS ➤

MISSING MASS · NOT TAKING COMMUNION · NEGLECTING CONFESSION DURING EASTER

➤ HOW TO BREAK THE SPELL ➤

· BE RECOGNIZED IN THEIR WOLF FORM · BE HUMBLED BY THEIR NAKEDNESS ·
· NEVER SPEAK OF THE INCIDENT ·

OR THROUGH THE ENDURING WILL OF THEIR HUMANITY

SURVIVES THE 101 DAYS WITHOUT SPILLING THE BLOOD OF AN INNOCENT OR KILLING ANOTHER PERSON

ROUX-GA-ROUX

IS A CREOLE VARIATION OF LOUP GAROU

SUFFER THE CURSE OF THE ROUX-GA-ROUX

· DOUBLE CROSS A WITCH · BREAK A PROMISE · FORGET A PLEDGE ·

➤ 101 NIGHTS! ➤

YOU WILL TRANSFORM INTO A RAVENOUS BEAST

HEAD OF A WOLF · ELONGATED LIMBS AND UNFATHOMABLE STRENGHTH · LONG CLAWS AS HARD AND SHARP AS A CLEAVER

YOU WILL PROWL THE SWAMPS IN SEARCH OF HUMAN PREY

➤ 101 DAYS! ➤

SHAMEFUL OF YOUR NIGHTLY RAMPAGES · FEARFUL OF BEING DISCOVERED · WEAK AND SICKLY · WEARY AND DISCONSOLATE

UNSATIATED AND EVER-HUNGRY FOR MORE FLESH AND BLOOD

⸱⸙ PAAKNIWAT ⸙⸱
WYOMING ∗ UNITED STATES

This water is a rainbow of orange and yellow shallows that blend into depths of green and turquoise – a beautiful deceit that disguises the hot pools of bubbling acidic water that rise to the surface from deep, subterranean reservoirs. The geysers of Yellowstone hiss and steam, erupting in awe-inspiring displays of the intense heat and power lurking below.

This is an ancient land that existed long before the United States and North America, and even long before the arrival of the different tribes of Indigenous peoples who settled in these rugged lands. Is it any wonder that those who claim this land as their home are just as ancient?

Below this majestic territory, hellfire rages. Within a massive caldera, molten rock ebbs and flows, pushing against the ground above only to recede again, heating the aquifer to beyond livable temperatures and infusing it with noxious gases and caustic minerals.

Within these volatile waters resides a race of beings that are beautifully delicate in appearance, yet also capable of withstanding the scorching heat and deleterious acidity of their habitat. Swimming to the surface, they wonder about the human creatures above, and sing songs of melancholic loveliness to lure us nearer to their gaze.

They are not a nefarious species, but their curiosity about humans can lead to catastrophic results. In their pursuit to know us better, they sing their songs of enchantment, bringing us closer and closer still. A mesmerism of sorts, hypnotic and bewitching, their beautifully painful melodies clasp onto our souls and seize our hearts, drawing us in. When we are upon them, standing precariously at the edge of the pool in their full view, we witness their beauty, too – their delicate forms, just below the surface of the water. As our eyes lock with theirs, our human heartbeats quicken and euphoria takes hold, our knees wobble and all stability is lost. In an instant of joy, our human bodies collapse, and we plunge into the scorching acidic waters. There is a moment of elation and bliss, before our skin burns and our flesh melts away to nothingness.

⊷⊷✺ TUKÁKAME ✺⊷⊷
WIRIKUTA DESERT ✳ MEXICO

As you make your way across the desert, the heavy sun sets and a sliver of moon hangs high above. Prairie dogs scurry to find homes as the last of the daylight fades, and the foxes cry to usher in the darkness of night. From the blackest crease in the darkness, a lone wolf emerges, his maw bloodied and his muzzle dripping from a recent kill. With his eyes fixed upon you, he lopes across the sand, moving in and out of the shadows. He enters a final shaft of darkness and this time, he does not return. Was he a mirage, a figment of your imagination? Or has he truly disappeared?

From the same patch of darkness into which the wolf vanished comes the rattle of dry bones, soft at first, then louder. There in the blackness of the shadow, two pinpoints appear, darker than the shade that surrounds them. They fix their gaze upon you. At last they blink, and below them the glimmer of sharp white teeth slowly emerge as if they are being unwrapped and presented with unabashed pride. A rattle of bones like maracas echo through the night as the pair of eyes advance toward you. Breaking from the edge of the darkness, you see a shock of hair, ragged and filthy with rope-stiff blood. Two coarsely broken and jagged horns jut angrily from the creature's brow, his soulless eyes – now fully visible – bulge from his taunt-skinned, grinning skull. The rattling continues, and you realize it is coming from the collection of bones hanging about his waist. Wings unfurl from his back as he takes to the air and lands, crouching, on a boulder just feet from where you sit. His lips pull back to reveal a ragged broken-tooth and blood-stained grimace.

The scent of him is unbearable – acrid flesh and fetidness. His hands are sticky with blood, rotten flesh is stuck in his long nails and his body is covered in filth. He tilts his head left to right, his dark eyes blinking rapidly, as if trying to understand the nature of you. Then all at once he pounces. Nails stab your skin and teeth gnash your bones, but fear not! He doesn't enjoy the taste of fresh flesh, so he won't consume you now, not on the spot. He will stash your corpse away for a while, and will return for his feast once you've had a chance to acquire a bit of rancidness.

ᵕ᷈ᔌᔦ᷈ EL SOMBRERÓN ᔧᕗᔦᔌᵕ

CHIAPAS * MEXICO

Silver buttons gleam in the late afternoon sun, pinpoints of brilliance sparkling on a charro that is smart and dustless yet somehow dull and ashen, not so much black as lacking in hue, its color as wearisome as the Devil's soul. There are boots to match, large and angular, which crush the gravel as silver spurs clank and jangle, punctuating each long stride with a slow and purposeful somber cadence. His handsome face, obscured by the shadow of his large black hat, is sharp and rugged, and a small mustache, turned up at the ends, runs across his upper lip. Although only the most courageous – or foolhardy – would dare to look his way, catching his glance can result in an incapacitating fear, leaving people frozen with trepidation, unable to speak, and overcome with an indescribable terror that can linger for days, weeks or even months.

He strolls through the village leading four mules, their raven manes and tails ornately braided, pulling a heavy load of shiny black coal. This is all simply a ruse to distract from his true intent – he wants the hand, body and soul of a beautiful young woman. He walks the darkened streets of the village looking for a maiden who will return his haunting glance.

When he finds her, he will tie his mules to a post in front of her house, pull out a silver guitar and begin to sing. This mesmerizing melody, the most beautiful sound the girl has ever heard, will capture her heart. When finished, El Sombrerón will quietly pack away his guitar, untie his mules and stroll away, leaving the lovelorn maiden alone in her heartbreak. For days she will be unable to eat, drink or sleep, trapped in an infatuation so intense it eclipses the basic requirements of life. Doctors will visit, prayers will be uttered, but nothing will break the spell of El Sombrerón.

Nights later, the maiden will hear the distant song of El Sombrerón again. Her heart will race as she sneaks out of her house in search of him, heedless of the rough gravel tearing her bare feet. When she finds him, she'll plead for his love, and beg to yield to his desires. Brushing her hair behind her ear and caressing her soft face, he will begin to sing again, slowly braiding her long dark hair as he does so. When he is finished, he will gently take her hand and lead her out of the village and into the darkness. They'll walk through the night, on to the next town where the ruse will begin anew, only this time, El Sombrerón will stroll in with five mules, their raven manes and tails ornately braided, pulling a heavy load of shiny black coal.

In the dense rainforest, humid air clings to leaves, then drips as water into pools on the ground. The thick canopy casts deep shadows, creating an eternal twilight. Here and there are small gaps in the foliage through which shafts of light break, streaking across the darkness. Light is a welcome visitor within this lonesome umbrage, offering a hopeful brightness and relief for tired eyes.

A human's nature is to find comfort in the familiar, and this is where the Tunda finds her strength and opportunity. Your trust in those you hold most dear is her greatest advantage.

For days she will observe you, watching from the darkness of the jungle, waiting to identify a person in whom you have absolute confidence. Then she will show herself, but not before shapeshifting in order to appear as this most beloved individual. For children, she will usually become the mother, and for those who are older, it will likely be a spouse, a friend or a lover. The Tunda will stand at the edge of the jungle motioning for you to come near. It's always the same – she will lure you close, and, taking your hand, will lead you into the forest. There, she will feed you shrimp and crab, lulling you into a docile state, convincing you completely that she is your loved one.

The Tunda's victims will never choose to leave her, not even after she reveals her true appearance – a bent and broken body, and a wrinkled face set with sunken, bulging eyes, like a fresh corpse that has just climbed out of a grave. She smells like a corpse too. Keeping her victims close, she will make you work and keep her company, until at last she tires of you. Then, transforming into a wild animal, the Tunda will violently consume you, before moving on to find her next victim.

The Tunda's one flaw is that her shapeshifting is often haphazard. She can't always seem to control every aspect of the change, and frequently a part of her will be glaringly imperfect. In some cases, one leg will be in the shape of a *molinillo* – a wooden kitchen utensil used to stir hot chocolate.

What the Tunda lacks in attention to esthetic detail, she makes up for in deceitful cunning. She disguises any defect, knowing that the recognizable will always distract from the unfamiliar.

CHICHIRICÚ
CUBA

The nocturnal jungle is alive with sound. Small animals scurry about, and a choir of insects sings. In the distance, a larger, more predatory creature bellows into the night, as if giving fair warning of its approach. In the darkness of these woods, the snap of a twig could be the result of a large mammal's footfall, or it could just as easily signal the arrival of a terrifying creature unknown.

Just as the Indigenous peoples who made the arduous journey to this land are cousins to those they left behind so long ago, so too are the Chichiricús cousins to the goblins and gnomes of the old world. Facing new hardships and threats on their travels, the Chichiricús had to adapt and evolve over time. They became leaner, stronger and more capable of hunting with just their hands, claws and teeth. They lived near water, and, still preferring the darkness of night over day, they spent most of the daylight hours slumbering just below the water's surface, only coming up for an occasional breath.

Their fearlessness and tenacity to protect what was theirs only grew stronger from one generation to the next. To them, this new land was paradise compared to the barren and frigid tundras of the north, and the Chichiricús were joyful in their new home, as well as aware of the danger of outsiders. This is their land, the night is their time, and here in the darkness, your unwelcome presence could be considered trespassing.

Chichiricús are often found playing near a body of water at night, dancing in the cascading rapids of a waterfall. Giggling and jovial, their long bodies slap the water's surface as they tumble from great heights in a jubilant display of aquatic acumen. The sight of them will fill you with an unimaginable delight, their childlike mannerisms and pure exuberance will lull you into a false sense of security.

At last, you allow yourself a laugh, a brief but audible giggle that stops short when you see a head turn, revealing two glowing eyes looking back at you. Then there are two more, and two more, until there are innumerable pairs of eyes staring at you from the darkness – burning embers as countless and voiceless as the stars overhead. The Chichiricús have stopped laughing, the sounds of their merriment now replaced by vicious whoops and hollers that precede your dying screams.

--⟨⟩ SOUCOUYANT ⟨⟩--
DOMINICAN REPUBLIC

She draws her curtains. The day is closing, and the sun sinks heavy toward the horizon. Now is not the time for slumber, at least not for her – now is the time to feed.

She runs her ragged-nailed finger from the base of the back of her neck, up over her head, down her brow and over her nose, lips and chin, slicing through her skin as it if were the rind of an orange. She continues over the contours of her neck and through the shallow valley of her breasts, down past her sagging belly to her abdomen. As easily as if she were removing clothes, she sheds her skin, starting at the head and ending with the legs and feet. Like a workman having taken off a soiled and dingy uniform, she wraps the wrinkled mass into a ball and places it in a mortar on a high shelf for safe keeping. Then she evaporates, subliming into a luminous green mist that passes into the night through a keyhole.

Tonight, perhaps it's Diaz's turn – he chased the cat with a broom just for the fun of it. Or maybe it's Señora Peña's time – she's always so unpleasant, and never says hello.

Finding a crack in a door, she presses though, drifting from room to room until she finds her victim – Diaz it is. Swirling around his sleeping form, she comes to rest on him, heavy like a blanket upon his body. Gently, on the inside of his arm, she punctures his skin with her teeth – blood flows, and there is rhapsody and euphoria within her. Drunkenly satiated, she pulls herself away before she drinks too much and takes his life. His skin will be black and blue by morning, but he will live.

Now she finds her way out, flying back to her home as a glorious green mist in the night. Unfolding her skin, she steps back in, one foot then the other, slipping her hands down through the arms and tugging them taut on the fingers. She adjusts the face just so, carefully fixing the jawline and the holes for her eyes.

Satisfied now, she lays her head down to sleep and thinks about who deserves a visit tomorrow night. Who will cross her before the next day's sun drops below the horizon?

·⟨⟩ MÈTMINWI ⟨⟩·

HAITI

Stars fill the sky and the first bell tolls . . . *gong*. The air is heavy with humidity ... *gong*. One tone after another . . . *gong* . . . like a countdown as pedestrians quickly make their way home . . . *gong*. Leaves rustle in the treetops along the boulevard . . . *gong*. Doors slam shut . . . *gong* . . . the shuffle of feet on gravel streets . . . *gong* . . . long nails scratching concrete walls . . . *gong*. Long fingers tap, tap, tapping . . . *gong*. Joints pop . . . *gong*. Bones grind as long legs flex . . . *gong* . . . GONG! The twelfth bell tolls, then . . . silence.

Fingers, slender and crooked, with nails broken and stained from recent victims, creep cautiously around stone quoins as Mètminwi, the "Master of Midnight," stalks his prey. A narrow head peers around the corner, forehead and brow pale and furrowed, with a knotted clump of bedraggled hair running across two red eyes. His craning neck clatters into place like a coarse chain unfurling as he looks around. He needs just one, but who would begrudge him his appetite if he were to happen upon two?

His rangy frame is impossible to conceal, yet he crouches in the shadows, gangly legs folded in the darkness, chin resting on bent knee, twisted and grimacing. He waits for the unfortunate stragglers running behind time, and for the staggerers, stumbling and joyous from too much drink. Midnight is his, as are those who dawdle in its starlight glow.

A bottle clanks against hard stone, and his head snaps as he looks toward the clattering source of the noise. He unfolds himself from the darkness like some great arachnid, joints snapping into place.

His bent and rickety frame, hunched and crooked, is nearly two stories in height. With arms outstretched from one building to another, he braces himself as he takes his first staggering, clumsy steps toward the commotion. He spies a fellow, drowsy from drink, falteringly tripping down the street. Moving on his victim as if he was a fly trapped in a web, Mètminwi's sinewy fingers snatch the man up mid-stride. There is a flurry of movement, a rush of pops and snaps. From a distance, there is a brief scream followed by the sound of breaking bones, viscous splitting and the smacking of lips. Then, there is nothing.

The bell tolls once again . . . *gong*. One a.m.

❧ MAMA D'LEAU ❧

DOMINICAN REPUBLIC

If only it were the case that the beautiful, natural state of this world was respected. We do try, most of us, to be good stewards with what little influence we have, but there are also those who seem truly incapable of looking at our vast home and seeing anything other than themselves; those who look at the wilderness and simply see unfulfilled potential, untamed lands that need to be conquered – a means to a profit.

We can never truly know what intentions live inside another person's heart, but deep in the wilds of the Dominican Republic, Mama D'Leau has made herself both judge and jury, and – if need be – executioner of those who do not respect the earth.

Come with an open heart, tread lightly and leave no sign of yourself where you go, and Mama D'Leau will bestow upon you all the wonders of this glorious planet's beauty. However, arrive with intentions of turning a quick profit from the world's resources, and she will place peril at every turn of your path. You will find that your way is often lost, thorns will clutch and tear at your skin, insects will bite and feed on your flesh – nature will be unbearable. In this Mama D'Leau is kindly offering you a warning, an opportunity to rethink. Retreat now, leave and live, or carry on with your malicious conduct and place your fate in her hands.

You know she is near when you hear her song. Among the lilt of forest birds, a subtle hum floats upon a breeze. When you see her, she appears as a beautiful woman bathing in a pond, vulnerable in her nakedness. Her long hair cascades over her shoulders, flowing across the surface of the water. Her hands delicately trace over the water, small whirlpools forming with every movement. All the greed and ambition that you once felt for the spoils of wild places is now entirely for her – for her beauty and purity. Mama D'Leau's innocence and perfect wonder is now your only focus.

Beguiled by her radiance, you will not notice that below the water her body is the long, scaly, speckled one of an anaconda. Nor will you feel the chill of her embrace as your hands reach for her. In the throes of desire, you will not feel her reptilian tail as it coils around your feet, your legs, your arms and torso, tightening and squeezing the air out of your body. With your breaths faltering, you will continue to marvel in the wonder of Mama D'Leau, even as you're drawn under the surface of her deadly pond.

❧ HEADLESS RIDER ❧

SANTA CLARA ✳ CUBA

The Ten Years' War – the fight for Cuban independence – saw extreme acts of barbarism from both sides. The revolutionaries attacked in the still of the night, fighting quietly with machetes and knives, and stealing rifles and ammunition from the corpses of the Spanish. The Spanish despised these tactics, and would enact extreme revenge on any rebels found with stolen Spanish weapons. One such vengeful Spaniard was a handsome young *capitán*, a son of the Spanish aristocracy. Unlike his comrades, who were driven to anger at the sight of Spanish weapons in rebel hands, he delighted in it. He believed that even with Spanish rifles, the Cubans were no match for the superiority of the Spanish .

The soldiers had just bedded down after a violent day. The stars shone bright overhead as the young *capitán* began to drift off to sleep. Awoken by the sudden unsettled neighing of Spanish horses in the distance, he realized the rebels were upon them. Grabbing his belt and scabbard, he mounted the nearest horse and rode fast towards Santa Clara, intending to alert the soldiers stationed in the city to the surprise attack. He was quickly overtaken by rebels, but with the city lights visible in the distance, he confidently prepared to fight. Instinctively his hand reached for his sword, but the blade was not there. The hairs on the back of his neck stood up. Where could his sword have gone?

Terror rose within him as he remembered that he had left his sword unsheathed at the head of his bedroll, and he knew his only choice was to surrender. His face was familiar to the rebels, though, and his cruel deeds on the battlefield were too well known – the only mercy he would see this night was that of a swift death. With a single violent swing of a Cuban machete, the *capitán*'s body was relieved of its head, which was quickly scooped up and placed in a bag as a trophy. His body was strapped to his horse, then sent galloping out into the night.

This was not the end of the handsome young *capitán*, though. He still rides for the city of Santa Clara, then races down Calle Maceo, sparks flying on the cobblestone street, his horse belching flames. A headless specter – a revenant of vengeance past – too proud to concede to death, and in search, perhaps, of his missing saber.

⋯⊱⊰ CIGUAPA ⊱⊰⋯
DOMINICAN REPUBLIC

The survey team had set up camp in a small clearing with daylight to spare, so the three men who had become fast friends during their arduous journey to the jungle decided to explore the area. With map in hand, they began to cut a path through the underbrush. As the trio forged ahead, machete slicing through the fallen branches and new growth, they could hear the sounds of flowing water mingled with an unusual melancholy noise, barely audible, almost like humming.

They came upon a small stream, and there in the light of the waning sun they saw a small woman, fully nude and in alluring recline, on a shallow ledge above a small reservoir. Although only four feet tall, her body was beautifully proportioned, finely featured and voluptuous. It must have been a trick of the fading light of day, but her skin seemed to glow a vibrant azure color. Sensually combing her long cobalt hair, she sang a heartrending melody in a minor key, her legs sultrily folded beneath her, hiding her backward-facing feet. The three friends, mesmerized, watched lustfully from behind the cover of jungle foliage.

As he locked eyes with her, the boldest of the three friends stood and began to make his way toward her. He felt a deep love and intense desire unlike anything he'd ever experienced before. Overcome with sudden jealousy, a second man rushed after his friend. Through pangs of love and imagined betrayal he ragefully swung his machete, striking from behind. So ferocious was the attack, his blade became lodged in the meaty tissue above his friend's collarbone, killing him almost instantly. As his friend's corpse fell to the ground in front of him, he raised his gaze to meet her's. Now as she stood on the ledge, her beauty was on full display. Her song so mesmerized the man that he didn't even notice that his throat had been slit from behind by the third of the party. Falling to his knees, the woman's melancholic tune mingling with the sound of blood gurgling from the massive gash in his throat, he bled out even as he continued to stare into her deep blue eyes.

The final man, captivated by the woman's bewitching cobalt gaze, stood motionless. Insouciantly stepping over his friends' corpses, she slid her small hand into his, and drew him toward her. Her song continued as, hand in hand, she led him deeper into the jungle, never to be seen again.

·✺·❦❀ EL DUENDE ❀❦✺·

MEXICO

Awakening in a nest made of filthy, unwashed hair, dry-bloodied bandages and nail clippings, his day begins when the lights of the house go out. After a yawn and a few lengthy stretches, he begins scurrying about the lath and plaster, his ragged sharp claws scratching within the darkness. Inside the walls, he climbs over the gnawed bones of a mouse and finds an old, dehydrated bat – a treat, but nothing compared to the harvest that awaits him beyond these boundaries. Out there is a miscellanea of tastes and smells, a smorgasbord of savory delicacies and delightful flavors. As he clambers from one room to another, he finds a fat, juicy house centipede – a quick snack before the feast, he gnashes his sharp teeth and crunches the insect up. Peering through a crack in the ceiling he spies the real prize – an unkempt boy, no more than seven, sleeping soundly in his bed. Oh, what a filthy delight!

Lithely descending the wall and scuttling across the floor to the head of the bed, he stealthily climbs toward the boy's musty hair – the scent of hay, tangy sour and barnyard sweet. Bits of dry skin pulled from the scalp make a wonderfully rank appetizer, the consistency of stale bread and the flavor of old shoes. Squeals of delight at a dirty ear – this is where the meal begins in earnest. He must take a delicate approach, as the slightest of sounds can waken even the heaviest of sleepers. Oh, but the joys of success – a jelly saccharine treat, a gummy brown-paste delicacy, the flavor of lamb's dung and barbacoa. An afternoon's perspiration dried on grimy skin, salty sweet with an unclean piquant.

At the foot of the bed he finds a main course – uncut toenails, jagged and dirt-packed. His sharp claws dig out a treacly gum with a chewy crunch, a pâté of pinworm egg, grime and fungus. He is euphoric at this feast of filthiness. "Surely no one would begrudge me just one toe . . . a meaty, thick-boned treat to tide me over until tomorrow's feast?" He snaps off a toe of lesser importance – the second from the last on the left foot – then hops off the bed, scrambles across the floor and scales the wall, his savory plunder tucked under his arm. He lays his head down to sleep, the boy's toe as a pillow, "This will tide me over," he thinks, "until tomorrow's sun fades and the feast begins anew."

⋯ DUPPY ⋯

JAMAICA

There were two shy Duppy that lived in the old shed where the garden tools were kept. They stayed in the dark corners when people were near, and would knock or sometimes push something over to make their presence known. If you didn't pay them any notice they'd leave you well enough alone, or if you said something kind, like, "Hello Duppy, fine day we're having," they might leave you a shiny gift – an old soda cap, a broken bit of gleaming mirror, or, now and again, an old coin shiny and new as the day it was minted.

Up in the old house though, there were at least five Duppy. There was one in the attic who, every so often, enjoyed a stomp around at night – moving boxes and furniture from one side of the room to the other, causing a ruckus. We'd storm up the stairs to see the cause of the disturbance and find nothing; everything was where it was supposed to be.

Two of them stayed in the back bedroom, which never got much light and had a certain gloominess about it. The darkness didn't seem to come from a lack of illumination, the room just felt dark. The Duppy didn't care about our comfort, so sleep in this room was fitful – dreams came too easily and lingered too long after you woke.

One stayed in the kitchen near the pantry, seeming to enjoy the smell of good cooking and the sight of us appreciating a good meal. On an occasional Sunday morning we'd inexplicably find the rum and treacle down from the cupboard, set on the counter ready for fresh banana fritters. If the request was ignored and none were made, there'd be a mess to clean up later in the day – flour spilled all over the counter, rice all over the floor, or cups and silverware tossed about the table.

In the cellar, there was a nasty Duppy. Spiteful and vicious, it took pleasure in unsettling us. As if the frightful darkness as you descended the stairs was not scary enough, a looming presence could always be felt there, ominously close, never more than a step behind you, ever pressing, until at last, in haste, you'd turn and run back up the stairs, emerging into the light of day once more.

···❦ CHUPACABRA ❦···

MOCA ∗ PUERTO RICO

It first began in the small village of Moca. Eight sheep, each with three deep punctures in their chests, were discovered with their bodies completely drained of blood, covered in an unusual viscous slime. At first, the villagers assumed that this must be the influence of Satan – perhaps there was a cult in their midst, performing devious acts to appease their dark master. But when no proof of this theory turned up, and more farms reported similar occurrences, the villagers' imaginations turned to a more sinister culprit. Tales of *el vampiro de Moca* quickly spread, and homes were soon adorned with wreaths of garlic and crucifixes, doors were given additional bolts, and windows were always locked at night.

As more killings occurred, the island of Puerto Rico erupted into a frenzied horror, the likes of which had never been seen before. Before long, however, locals started to have sightings of the creature that was wreaking havoc.

Near the town of Canóvanas, a farmhand was driving goats home when he saw a creature stalking his herd just off in the brush. Noticing that it was walking on all fours, he believed it to be a wild dog, so he ran toward it, hollering and yelling in the hope of scaring it off. As he neared his target, it rose onto its two hind feet and faced him. The sight of it stopped the farmhand in his tracks, his mind screaming to flee, his body frozen, until all at once the creature fell to the ground and scampered away. That same night, further down the road, several caged rabbits, two dozen chickens and a few turkeys were found dead, bled dry, with three puncture wounds.

It was near dusk when another townsman went out to check on his family dog who was barking incessantly. He rounded the corner of his home, and that's when he saw it – hunched over and snatching at the dog: a diminutive reptilian creature, scaly and green, with large, slanted red eyes that glowed intently in the dusk. Running down its hunched spine, from its head to the small of its back, were sharp quills, splayed like a porcupine's. It hissed and croaked, clawed and tore, grabbing until at last it had the terror-stricken dog in its grasp. Lifting the dog toward its flat face, a tube-like appendage suddenly projected from a small orifice near the creature's chin. The dog yelped as its master hurled several fist-sized stones. One stone found its mark, the creature stumbled backward, let out a craggy bellow and fled on all fours into the undergrowth. The frightened dog was fine, save the three puncture wounds in its neck.

LOS AVISTAMIENTOS

1975: MOCA – PUERTO RICO

It all started with the death of 15 cows, swiftly followed by the death of a small herd of goats, a few geese, and a pig. All were found dead in the fields, a pattern of triangle marks on their necks and their bodies drained entirely of all blood. At first, the community feared a vampire, and tales of el vampire de Moca quickly spread. Some suspected there was a Satanic cult in their midst. As more and more bloodless corpses were found, the townsfolk were whipped up into a frenzy. It all came to a head when a man claimed to be attacked by a large creature covered in feathers. He threw stones at it to try and scare it away but it only turned and attacked him.

1994: PUERTO RICO

A farmer from the far western side of Puerto Rico found a nest of four small, strange-looking, grey-and-white-feathered reptile creatures with little round mouths in his barn. He used a pitch-fork to chase them, screaming and crying, out into the dark.

AUGUST 1995: CANOVANAS – PUERTO RICO

A creature with large red eyes and hairy arms was seen trying to break through a window of a home. The witness claimed the creature bristled when it realized it had been seen, its coarse feathers standing up along its spine, before it turned and ran off into the night. Over the next few weeks, more than a dozen turkeys, a small herd of goats, cows, several of the village's feral cats and dogs, and even a horse were all found dead, with not a single drop of blood left in their corpses. In the month of August alone, more than 150 animals were found dead in the village. Back at the house where the attempted break-in had occurred, a rancid chunk of white meat was found covered in a puddle of slime, and a small animal stuffed toy was found torn to shreds, as if it had been seen as prey.

DEL CHUPACABRAS

1995: OROCOVIS – PUERTO RICO

A small farming community was horrified to find the corpses of eight dead sheep in a field one day. Each of the animals had been completely drained of their blood, and each had three strange puncture holes in their chest.

NOVEMBER 1995: CANOVANAS – PUERTO RICO

A creature ran from the jungle and attacked a dog in front of its owner. The man ran to his dog's defense, only to have the creature turn on him instead. Despite being only four feet tall, the creature flexed as if prepared to fight, with what looked like feathers or quills standing up all along its back. The man picked up a large branch as the creature's mouth opened and a long tubular shaped appendage extended out and toward the ground. The creature then turned and ran back into the rough.

DECEMBER 1995: GUANICA – PUERTO RICO

More animals – mostly livestock and rabbits – were brutally killed throughout December, and all were found drained of their blood. One of the animals discovered was a large cat, with the telltale three puncture marks not in its neck, but directly through its skull. Some strange, three-toed claw tracks were found near some of the corpses.

DECEMBER 1995: GUANICA – PUERTO RICO

In the early hours of the morning, Osvaldo Rosado was washing his car when he was suddenly grabbed forcibly from behind. As he fought to free himself from his attacker, he felt sharp talons slice into his abdomen. As he turned, he found himself face to face with a large, red-eyed creature that was covered in sharp spines and had a strange round mouth that protruded from its face. After Rosado struck the creature in the eye, it squealed and ran off into a nearby wood.

☞ THE ROLLING CALF ☜

JAMAICA

There are those who can see it, and there are those who cannot, but either way, you will know when the Rolling Calf is there.

The physical manifestation of the soul of a truly evil and despicable person, the Rolling Calf has been condemned to wander the country roads. This cruel being inflicts unease and misfortune on anyone who may cross its path. Haunting forests, caves and other abandoned places, it never ceases to search for the souls of the innocent and the sinful alike.

You will hear the Rolling Calf's approach long before you see it – the clanging and clanking of a chain – a foreboding sound that is said to instill a paralyzing fear into all who hear it. Then two eyes appear, glowing like red-hot coals burning in the blackness of night. And finally, slowly ambling out of the darkness will come a white, hornless goat, a massive beast, as tall and strong as a bull. Fettered around the neck, its lock and chain drag along the dusty ground behind the creature. Flames burn within the animal's nostrils, creating sickly fumes and a smell of sulfur and decay that will overwhelm you.

As if this is not enough, the beastly creature's front legs are themselves a disturbing abomination – the right leg is like that of a large man, while the left leg is like that of horse. The Rolling Calf is a loathsome and revolting sight, and if you cannot break from its frightful spell, it will tear you limb from limb, stomping you into a pasted mush of broken bone and flesh, blood and dirt.

To escape the beast, you must make your way to a crossroads, across which the wicked and dishonest soul will not be able to pass. Some say that casting rice on the ground will confuse the beast, stopping it in its tracks. A tarred whip wielded in your left hand will also keep this evil manifestation at bay. But be aware that even if bested, the animal will return again and again. It will remember your face, and will seek vengeance in a moment when you least expect it.

EL JACHO CENTENO

OROCOVIS * PUERTO RICO

Reaching down into a small cup, he pulls out a wriggling waxworm and spears its meaty body onto a fishhook. He casts it out over the calm waters of the small pond, and moments later a fish pulls hard on the line, fighting. He reels it in quickly, and pulls the fish to shore. This happens again and again – the fish bite, he reels them in. Afternoon soon becomes evening, and daylight yields to dusk. His enthusiasm has kept him out later than planned, and now he has to find his way home through the darkness.

He lights a *jacho* – a torch made of resinous wood soaked in oil, and begins the long walk home. Making his way through the darkness of the jungle, he stumbles along over gnarled root and fallen branch, with the nightjar's caw and the chuck-will's whoops and howls echoing in the distance.

The songs of crickets ring through the air as his *jacho* begins to fade, and with it his view of the path ahead. Pausing for a moment he searches among his bags for another source of light – anything that might burn and provide a bit of illumination – yet with little luck, all he found was a small wooden crucifix. He knows the dangers of the jungle at night, and, desperate for light, he reluctantly holds the tip of the crucifix to the dying flame. The dry wood bursts into flame, and once again he is on his way home. Soon, he is seated by the warmth of his hearth, enjoying a meal of the day's catch.

Days later, he suddenly falls ill and quicky dies. As a good Christian man, he finds himself at the gates of heaven expecting an eternity of salvation, but instead he is met with an inquiry over the burning of his crucifix. At the end of his appeal, a celestial verdict is read, he is condemned, and his punishment is delivered – he is tasked with collecting all the ash that fell from the burning of his sacred cross, and he must retrace his steps from beginning to end and back again until the whole crucifix is reconstructed.

It is said that to this day, a light can be seen floating through the jungle, bobbing about close to the ground and then back up again. So let this be your reminder to always be aware of your surroundings, and to always return home before the darkness of night overtakes the day.

EL ARBOL DEL VAMPIRO

GUADALAJARA * MEXICO

By the mid-eighteenth century, Guadalajara had grown to become one of the main population centers of New Spain. The city was flourishing culturally, and attracted architects, philosophers, scientists and writers from Europe. One such man was a Spanish grandee named Jorge. He acquired a hacienda and took to throwing lavish fiestas, inviting the cream of society. These opulent affairs would carry on all night and into the morning, but when the sun rose, the master of the manor was always nowhere to be found.

As time passed, the ranchers and farmers who lived near Jorge's hacienda noticed an increase in the number of livestock they were losing. One morning, when half a dozen spring calves were found each with two punctures in their neck and their blood drained from their bodies, a panic took hold of the community. Days passed and more corpses were discovered, so guard dogs were procured, only to be found cowering in fear. The night watch ran from one baying animal to the next, each time arriving only to find a fresh corpse, still warm. It was only when a local witch was consulted that the ranchers discovered what they were up against – there was a vampire in their midst . . . and all eyes turned to their new neighbor, Jorge. The witch told the group that in order to put an end to the community's suffering, they would have to stab Jorge through the heart with a stake made from the wood of a camichin tree.

The following morning, they stormed Jorge's hacienda, and found him sleeping in the cellar. They did as the witch had told them, and as they plunged the stake into his chest, Jorge cried out, vowing that in time he would return to seek revenge on their children's children's children.

With the stake still in his chest, the ranchers buried Jorge's corpse upside down, deep within the soil, then placed a massive stone over his tomb. However, the stone – meant to secure Jorge in his tomb – cracked open his coffin, allowing the camichin stake to begin to sprout.

The camichin eventually grew enough to break the ground above Jorge's tomb, and the magnificent tree now stands at more than 60 feet high. Time has been kind so far, but the locals fear that if the tree ever falls, Jorge will return . . . and this time, rather than hunting livestock, he will hunt humans.

·~❧3 EL CONQUISTADOR FANTASMA ჵ~·

MEXICO CITY * MEXICO

Car horns blare, trucks clatter over exposed cobblestone. A pickup rumbles by, its bed full of old appliances and metal scraps, *"Cualquier chatarra vieja a la venta!"* This city is no longer mine, and I do not recognize these people. Even this language they speak, although familiar, is not one I know.

Yet I recognize this tree, its creaks and groans. It gazes at me, a familiar sight. It stands sentry over me.

How many years have I stood at my post, phantom guard to this alley, invisible to the crowds that pass by here, unaware of my watch? Even if I wanted to, I could not stop them in their daily pursuits. *"Aguaaaaaaaaaaa, aguaaaaaaa!"* a man yells in the distance. This I also remember – "water." The sound of the word taunts me now. How long it has been since I felt the coolness of water on my throat! This curse, it seems, is mine to own. It is self-inflicted, arising from a choice I made myself all those years ago. And so I stand guard still.

So, too, does this tree. Branches spreading wide, quietly casting dark shadows, I know it judges me. I ask its forgiveness, yet it will not reply.

I had no idea he was so fragile. This sturdy young boy was capable and strong, he should have been able to take a tumble. Day after day, he asked his incessant questions, asking about the weight of my blade, wondering over the shine of my cuirass . . . 10, 20, 30 times a day he'd ask me something. Until finally, in a moment of exhaustion, I acted according to a impulse. A single swing of my hand, which was clad in metal, and he was broken, lying still on the ground. But how could I ever have known he was so fragile?

Cradling his lifeless body, I wondered how this was even possible. Just a moment ago he had been so lively. I nailed him to the avocado tree in order to ask his forgiveness eye to eye. His lifeless gaze gave me no clemency, but in his silence there was a judgment. So here I stand, under the dark foliage of this unforgiving tree: an invisible sentry, desolate and inconsolable, guarding the shadows of the past, unseen by the present.

⚜ EL CHARRO NEGRO ⚜
CHATUMAL ∗ MEXICO

Growing up in a family of very limited means, much of the boy's childhood was spent laboring to earn money to put food on the table and keep a roof over their heads. Want is a terrible unkindness for a child.

When the young man reached maturity, he left his parents' house determined to make a greater success of his own life. He believed he had a better chance of living well by himself than he did living at home.

As it turned out, though, it was not easier on his own. In fact, when success didn't come quickly enough for his liking, his pride made it even harder to bear. In his desire for nice things, he skipped meals and instead spent his money on fine clothing. He worked long hours so that he could acquire luxury. Yet as time passed, no amount of money seemed to make him happy, and he resented that his hands were always covered in dirt. He had prayed to God for wealth without result, so one night in desperation, he found himself kneeling in the dirt begging for help from the Devil instead.

Ol' Satanás must have giggled with glee when he heard the young man's plea and the desperation in his prayers, and when he appeared, he played hard into the boy's pride. Bowing his head, he offered, "How may I be of service?" When their interaction was complete, the young man had more money than he could spend in a hundred lifetimes, with the promise of more if he needed it, and the Devil left with a contract for the boy's soul when, as is the natural course of things, his time on earth came to an end.

The boy wasted no time in striking out for the nearest dance hall. He danced the night away, spending money on anyone who befriended him, drinking until the sun rose. Expensive new clothing came next, then a fine horse and a hacienda. With a lack of money no longer holding him back, the young man's tastes became more lavish. Women and gambling, fine clothing, drinking and feasting – there was nothing he couldn't buy. Even when he met with resistance, money always found a way. Limitless joy and pleasure were only ever as far out of reach as a chest full of silver and gold for this wealthy man. There was only one thing that seemed unobtainable: love. Those around him ate his food, drank his wine, laughed at his jokes and even slept in his bed, but he knew that if the wealth was not there, it was unlikely that they would care much for him.

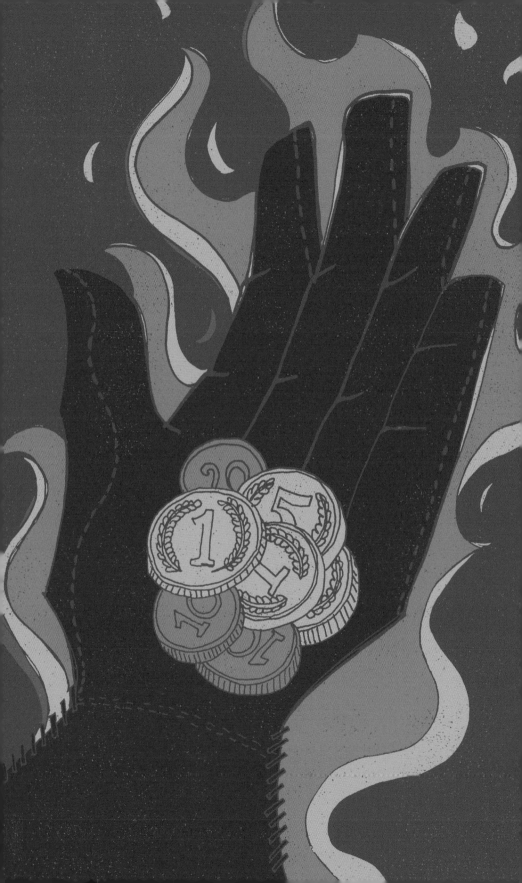

One afternoon, a man in a plain black suit sat in the wealthy man's front parlor. As he bowed his head and spoke, his identity became clear. It was the Devil, checking in to offer a friendly reminder of their deal. After complimenting the wealthy man's success, the Devil vanished in a cloud of brimstone and sulfur. The short visit played on the wealthy man's mind, just as the Devil knew it would. Where there had once been a lifetime of pleasures remaining, the man was suddenly concerned with every small ache, and every new wrinkle. His time was fleeting and he knew it. He gave up drinking, prayed incessantly, and even began to sleep in a small chapel, but none of these measures eased his fear of the inevitable.

One evening, in his desperation, the rich man plotted an escape from his unholy contract. If he went on the run and never spent two nights in the same place, how would the Devil find him? With his best horse and a bag of gold coins, he set off into the darkness. Galloping through the night, he came upon the Devil standing at the side of the road. The cocky ol' demon gave him a wave as the man pushed his steed on by. Further down the road, there was the Devil again, this time offering the tip of a hat and an evil, mocking grin. The rich man rode on and there he was in the middle of the road – that ol' Devil, arms outstretched from one ditch to the other.

The man realized that his time had come. The Devil gave a courteous nod and held out his hand, but the rich man's horse reared up and kicked at the Devil. Enraged, the Devil stomped his cloven foot to the ground, opening a great crevasse in the earth that lead straight to hell. "Your steed is brave," he bellowed, "perhaps more so than you, so the two of you will journey to hell together." Then, in his anger, a new idea came to him, and he said, "Or, you can remain here for now and collect the debts owed to me. If anyone accepts your offer of gold, you may bring them here to me, and I will allow them to take your place." The rich man's flesh immediately began to desiccate, and his eyes sunk into his grimacing skull like two smoldering embers. His skin clung to his bones as his black charro suit hung loosely from his skeletal frame. His horse, too, decayed as fire rose from its eyes, flames bursting forth as it exhaled.

El Charro Negro now rides every night in search of someone, driven like him by greed, to accept his bag of gold. Someone who might, in a moment of covetousness, take the weight of riches off El Charro Negro's weary back, and take his place riding endlessly though the darkness, night after night, collecting the debts of lost souls.

⸙ LA VIEJA CHICHIMA ⸙

VERACRUZ ∗ MEXICO

Far off in the solitude of the dense jungle, she makes her home in a crooked little house with a palm-thatched roof. Away from the prying eyes of neighbors, she lives among the snakes and lizards, and the large spiders discourage the kinds of visitors who might mind the mischief she gets up to.

She has lived a long life, and the years have not been kind to her. She has a bent and twisted back, hunched from years of heavy lifting, which creaks when she stands, each bone slowly snapping into place. Gnawing on bone and chewing gristle have cracked and worn her teeth, leaving only a few rotten molars and several long fangs protruding below her cracked lips. Her breasts hang low, so she often tosses them one over each shoulder to lighten the strain of their weight on her twisted frame. Her legs are so turned around and bent that she sleeps leaning on a wooden crutch; if she were to lay down, she wouldn't be able to get back up. But do not allow this weak and infirm appearance to lull you into a false sense of security. Her strength is great and her temperament irascible.

Early in the morning, before the heat of the day has come, crafty Veija Chichima goes into her yard and begins to fry plantains. She chooses only the ripest fruit with the darkest skin to ensure that the sugary-sweet scent of frying plantains will carry, wafting over hill and valley, forest and field for miles and miles, enticing small children with the smell of the crispy sweet treat. This devious old woman is not just hoping to lure any old children to her house, she's hoping for fine young plump children, those who run off in search of a stranger's food without asking their parents' permission – unkempt and ill-behaved, impolite and unruly.

When the children first arrive at her fence squawking and hollering, begging for the delicious snack, she initially denies them. She tells them that she couldn't possibly; she mustn't give them food because she doesn't know them, she doesn't know their parents, and surely, their parents would not allow it. All the while, the devious old wretch keeps a close watch on the children as she continues to fry the plantains to delectable perfection, snatching quick glances out of the corner of her eye. She parades a full platter of the perfectly crisp fruit directly in front of the little ones as they watch through her fence, hands wrapped around metal pickets as if prisoners to their yearning sweet teeth. She places the

feast on the table, which is also set with fresh cinnamon-sweet *orxata de xufa*, and again the pleas ring out: "Surely you must know me!" "My parents let me eat with the neighbors anytime!" "Please, I can do whatever I like as long as I'm home for dinner!" Vieja Chichima has heard them all before, but now she knows she has the children just where she wants them. She turns and looks directly at the children and says, "Well, I suppose it'll be okay just this once."

Unlocking her front gate, the children race to the table and dig in. They're quick to fill their plates, unrestrained and riotous, and the whole scene soon becomes an uproarious and mannerless feast. The jungle erupts with the clank of forks and knives on plates, and the clink of glasses raised for more *orxata*. Nothing is spared, and when all's eaten – plates licked clean, and crumbs eagerly swept up and into open mouths – the affair is still far from over. Having gorged themselves on sweets and cinnamon-honeyed milk, the children fly into sugar-induced jollification. Bounding about in vigorous play, they kick balls and chase one another from one side of the yard to the other. It's only a matter of time until they all begin to wind down, the sugar wearing off, then one after another they all lay down for a nap, finding cozy places among the grass to rest a little.

This is the moment when crafty Vieja Chichima goes to work, snatching up one child after another, taking them into her house. Some she gently tucks between thick sheets of pastry, dusting them with chili, oregano and cumin before quickly pinching together the edges and slipping them into the oven. Others are stripped of their dingy clothing and then tossed into a giant pot of onion, tomato and chilis, where they'll stew for several days. The skinniest of the children will be kept for a month or two, and will be fed fried plantains and *orxata* until they've plumped up, then they too will find their themselves cooked up as part of one of Vieja Chichima's meals.

BRUJAS Y BRUJOS

BE WARY OF NOCTERNAL MEANDERINGS OF TURKEYS

Hidden in a windowless room of their homes brujas y brujos secretly remove their legs and take the form of turkeys. Unrecognizable to their neighbors they hunt through the dark hours of night looking for children to suck blood from. If you find a bruja's hidden legs and destroy them in fire, the bruja, unable to reattach her legs, will die by morning.

BRUJAS BLANCAS

A WHITE WITCH PRACTICES GOOD SPELLS
WORKS AS A CURANDERA PROVIDING
HERBAL MEDICINES AND FOLK HEALING
CAN REMOVE AND EVEN REVERSE
HARMFUL SPELLS SENDING THEM
BACK TO THE ONE WHO CAST THEM

BRUJAS NEGRAS

A BLACK WITCH ACCEPTS PAYMENT
TO CAST MALICIOUS SPELLS FOR
THOSE WHO SEEK VENGENCE OR
INTEND TO DO HARM
THEY PRACTICE IN THE DARK
ARTS AND BLACK MAGIC

LA LENGUA DE LAS BRUJAS

A BRUJA'S TONGUE TAKES THE SPINDLY AND SILKY FORM OF A SPIDER WEB AT NIGHT
FLOATING LIGHTLY ON THE AIR IT TRAVELS THROUGH THE OPEN WINDOW
CUT WITH AN IRON SCISSORS IT WILL TURN BACK INTO THE BRUJA'S SEVERED TONGUE

TAKE CAUTION!

• SALT THE ROOF • SLEEP WITH IRON SCISSORS OPEN AS A CROSS BENEATH THE BED •
• NEVER SAY "BRUJA" ON A FRIDAY •

·❀3 EL CUCUY ❀·
MEXICO

The glare of headlights sweep across the room through an open window. A hazy shaft of brightness bending around corners and chasing shadows from one side of the room to the other, casting a long, dark shadow across the closet door. Slightly ajar, the door slowly creaks open as if the house were taking a deep breath, then slowly creaks back again as it seemingly exhales. Blankets are pulled high over heads as the door creaks open and then slowly shuts once again. The mind reels as another car drives by, washing the room with light once again as shadows dash for corners and cower behind shelves, shrinking momentarily, only to reclaim the room as darkness returns.

Long nails scratch along a wooden door, red eyes peer from out of the darkness, glaring patiently across the room at a child sleeping soundly in his bed. El Cucuy blends seamlessly with the shadows that are cast across the bedroom floor. As if made of viscous black ink, he oozes his way beneath the slumbering child. He deeply inhales the intoxicatingly sweet smell of a freshly bathed boy, clean night clothes and freshly washed bedding. His wiry fingers, knotted and twisted, creep expectantly around the edge of the bedframe, over bedsheets and under pillows. The creature's eyes widen at the sight of mussed hair, still damp from the evening's bath. With his lips pulled back over his gaping mouth he takes another deep breath – the taste of shampoo and soap rushes past his sharp teeth and over his tongue. He is so close, but this is not the night, patience ... soon. A flick of the tongue, a quick taste of earlobe, and he's gone, seeped back into shadow and back to his closet retreat.

The following days are filled with mounting evidence. A tantrum over a denied piece of cake, pulling his little sister's hair, a pile of now-broken toys. In the closet hideaway, El Cucuy hears it all, confirmation of his suspicions. With all the evidence laid bare, a judgment is rendered, and now El Cucuy waits for daylight's passing and the inevitable approach of the night's darkness.

All is quiet now, save the creaking groans of an old house falling into slumber. Parents asleep down the hall, a disappointingly sweet little sister in the bedroom next door. But here, just beyond this closet door, is a sleeping boy, ill-mannered and grotty from the day's bad behavior, steeped in naughtiness and deep in his dreams.

A door latch clacks as the closet door moans on its hinges, opening slowly with the quietest of whimpers. The room is dark tonight, apart from the dim illumination creeping in from the hall. El Cucuy slinks along the baseboard, steadily inching his way to the foot of the bed. A clump of tangled, soiled hair and two beady red eyes peek stealthily over the edge and down the length of the bed, surveilling the task ahead. He slithers his way up and over the foot of the bed, and clambers over the covers until he's inches away from the child – succulent-sweet, sweaty-sour, and covered in the sickly smell of disobedience. In a moment, the boy is stuffed in a bag, tossed over a shoulder, and taken. Out to the hall, down the stairs, through the foyer, out the front door, into the street and gone – taken by El Cucuy.

He tears open the sack, and the child screams with fear at the sight of him. El Cucuy screams mockingly back as he wiggles his large, pointed ears – batlike and hair covered, they shift back and forth. The boy screams again, much to the mad elf's delight. El Cucuy leans in close and mockingly screams again. Misshapenly crooked, he dances a maniacal circling jig as screams beget screams in an unsettling game of call and response, until the sobbing begins. He bends down, slowly outstretching his knotted fingered hand and strokes the boy's head. Head tilting slightly, his eyebrows raise as his lips pull back and curl slightly. "Now, now, little man, you've been quite a loutish young hooligan," he croaks through his sharp-toothed grimace. "It has been such a delight, but now your ride's been ridden and a fare is due." His long tongue, pointed and scraggly, runs the full length of his upper teeth as he pulls his shoulders back and bares his palms.

Before another thought is given, he sinks his sharp, sharp teeth deep into the boy's flesh. One chomp, two chomp, three chomp, gone.

EL ORIGEN IMPÍO DEL CUCUY

It's believed that the name El Cucuy is derived from the Portuguese word for skull or head – and the direct translation comes from coconut, which was often used as a synonym for skull. The creature himself has many names, El Cucuy, Coco, Coca, Cuco, Cucu and Cucui, however, once you've caught his attention, it doesn't matter what you call him.

The first use of the name El Coco appeared in a play written in the early sixteenth century, Auto da Barca do Pargatorio, and it was a name used when speaking of the Devil himself.

Another tale of this character's transition from coconut to boogeyman comes from a Mexican legend:

A man, suffering from tuberculosis, is facing his final days. He is gaunt, withered and only steps away from death's door. He has been to doctors, priests and even a bruja or two, but none have given him any relief. In a final act of desperation, he seeks the help of a different bruja, one known not only for her success, but also for her dark and nefarious ways. She gives him a potion that will cure his disease and give him back the years of life he so desires, but there is a catch. For the potion to work, she says, he also has to drink the blood of children. He happily, greedily drinks the potion, but resists the second condition.

In the following days, his thirst grows as the disease continues to ravage his body. The potion he has taken, meant to be his cure, isn't working. As his limbs wither even further, the skin that once stretched over them fades, and hangs translucent and loose. All his teeth fall out, and his bloodied maw sprouts new, jagged ones in their place. As his appearance worsens, he takes to hiding in the shadows, not wanting to be seen by the townsfolk, and eventually, he moves to a cave on the outskirts of the village. As he is leaving town, his hunger gets the best of him, and, when he spots a child out past their curfew in the darkness of night, he thinks, "Just this once." He stuffs the poor boy in a bag, before running off to the darkness of his cave to devour his prey.

The Sierra Madre Oriental mountain range is on the eastern side of Mexico. More than 20 million years ago, earthquakes and volcanic activity pushed these ancient rocks upward, spilling magma from central Mexico all the way to the gulf. Over the centuries, many things have adapted and evolved, while others have remained unchanged.

Older than the land itself, it is said that the Ixoxoctic found his way to the surface in a gush of molten lava, was cast far into the sky, then fell back to earth as a massive meteor. Due to the great atmospheric friction, his skin crystalized in a firestorm of scorching heat. His descent ended with enormous force in the hills of Hidalgo, where he lay semi-molten in a huge crater of his own impact's making, glowing white hot until the rains began to fall, flooding his basin with deep, cold water.

This pool became his home. Over the eons he watched from beneath the water as the first small plants grew, followed by trees. Next was the arrival of small creatures, then larger ones – first leathery and hard, then covered in hair. Occasionally surfacing in a great whirlpool, he sometimes snatched up the animals who lingered too long at the edge of his pool. Eventually, humans arrived, taking to the hills that rose up around his basin. He watched them as they evolved.

In time, his home was given a name – Laguna de Azteca – and villages and even small cities sprang up around it. And yet the Ixoxoctic has not changed, at least not in form. His appetite has changed, or, more precisely, his cravings have. Fish are simply a snack these days, and small mammals a mere filler; it's the flesh of people that excites him – the sweet meat of humans that he craves.

A great whirlpool forms and from within it, he surfaces. Scanning the shore, his emerald eyes make contact with those of his victim. Deep and infinite as ocean waters, the Ixoxoctic's eyes hypnotize his unsuspecting prey as he slowly rises and moves toward them. His crystalline skin sparkles in the moonlight, peridot green and faceted, sharply ridged and hard-edged. His long arms reach out, and his sharp obsidian nails gouge deep into the human's flesh. With a quick jerk and a rapid twist, he's gone, and with him his meal. A large splash, then nothing.

CUIDADO
CON EL MAL DE OJO

PROTECT YOUR CHILDREN · PROTECT YOUR LOVED ONES · PROTECT YOURSELF

BEWARE THE EVIL EYE

MIND THE ENVIOUS GLANCE · A HATEFUL STARE · THE DISDAINFUL LEER · A LUSTFUL OGLE

RESIST THE MALEVOLENT GAZE WITH RED RIBBON SEWN INTO YOUR HEM
CARRY THE MANO DE AZABACHE – THE JET-BLACK HAND

➤ MIND THE ◄

RINGING IN YOUR EARS

SOMEONE IS SPEAKING ILL OF YOU

BITE YOUR TONGUE TO KEEP THEIR ILL INTENTIONS AT BAY
KEEP A CLOSE WATCH ON YOUR ENEMIES AND
AN EVEN CLOSER WATCH ON YOUR FRIENDS

DO NOT SWEEP AFTER THE SUN HAS SET!

AS YOUR SWEEPINGS ARE TOSSED OUT · MISFORTUNE WILL TAKE THEIR PLACE

⸭⸙ WA WA PACH ⸙⸭
YUCATAN ∗ MEXICO

As you go deep into the jungle, and then deeper still, trees of every variety possible grow one on top of another. Broad leaves sprout from the earth, stretching toward the hazy light that filters through the dense shade of the leaves overhead. The ground is a tangled mass of tree root and damp detritus, teaming with centipedes, ants and other crawling insects. Spiderwebs dangle from branches, while a thick blanket of moss clings to trunks and branches. Monkeys howl from the canopy above, while birds flit around the undergrowth. Thick and unforgiving, dense and lush, one could not imagine a wilder land than this.

Unseen by the naked eye are the vast number of creatures who call this jungle home – there are those who stalk far above the canopy, and those who slither along stealthily through the brush. Some animals are shrouded by the dark shadows of dense growth, some are hidden in the open, camouflaged by their hue and texture. The threatening nature of these living beings cannot be assessed by their size alone. Some of the tiniest creatures deep in the jungle here pose the greatest threat – a single bite or sting could cause an unsuspecting victim a host of dreadful ailments. While the largest animals use their ferocity and strength to create mayhem, other creatures, more devious ones, find concealment to be their most threatening tactic.

Wa Wa Pach is tall and lean, and his skin is gray and coarse. He stands with his long knobbed and twisted legs astride the paths of the jungle, with his large feet sunk into the detritus either side of the trail. His thin arms stretch out wide among the foliage of the canopy, his fingers, knotted and rough, intertwine with twig and branch as he bends his long, knurled head toward the ground and waits patiently. When his unsuspecting prey walks along his trail, paying little mind to the flora and fauna that surrounds them, they might easily mistake his limbs for the trunks of trees.

As his victim wanders beneath his long unseen legs, the Wa Wa Pach ensnares them between his gangly limbs. He presses and squeezes the breath out of his target, his slender fingers tangling and twisting around them, breaking bone and softening flesh until at last, in choking gulps, they are consumed.

⠂⠶❦ LA MALA HORA ❦⠶⠂
CHIAPAS ＊ MEXICO

While traveling the lonely back roads of rural North America during the darkness of night, all too often we encounter unusual occurrences that can test our belief systems. What we can easily dismiss during the light of day can, during the dark of night, become a constant nagging of uncertainty – with every turn comes another moment of unease. Road conditions, an occasional animal dashing out from the brush, and even just the simple task of staying awake, fighting off the monotony of the road, all add their toll. Alone in the dark, you race across open land, a ship in a vast sea of night. This is her time – the moment that La Mala Hora chooses to appear.

La Mala Hora is a dark entity who preys on those who are adrift in the desolate night. Her name, directly translated, is "the bad hour," but she is known by many as "the Evil Hour," or "the Evil One." According to some, she is more feared than the Devil himself.

To the traveler wandering the lonely back roads on foot, La Mala Hora appears as a solitary woman in a long black dress. With pale white skin, and long, knotted and tangled hair, she glides along just off the side of the road, her feet hanging below her, but not touching the ground. Her eyes are deep red, and it is said by some that if you meet her gaze, even for a moment, you could be driven insane with fear. Others claim that La Mala Hora's gaze can paralyze her victims into a form of hypnotic complacency, giving them the urge to follow her. It's in these instances that, if they are unable to regain control of their senses, they may find themselves led to the edge of a ravine or cliff, where they'll meet an untimely demise.

For those racing along the back roads and highways in the comfort of an automobile, La Mala Hora poses a more heartbreaking misfortune. Seeing her first along the side of the road she may be easily overlooked, but when her same stark figure shows up a few miles later and then again even further down the road her presence becomes impossible to ignore. It's when she appears, hovering in the middle of a crossroads or a fork in the road that their fate is sealed. Although no physical harm will come to the traveler, when eye contact is made an anxious trepidation and a longing for home will wash over them. In this moment La Mala Hora, the bad hour and dark omen poses no threat to the driver but foretells of the unforeseen death of someone dear to them.

~❧ EL SILBÓN ❧~
MEXICO

His whistle breaks the muggy silence of the late summer twilight. A somber tune first climbs and then drops back down the scale, until he reaches the final, unnerving note. Impossibly drawn out, the noise causes cats to hiss and dogs to cower beneath tables.

His clothes ragged from years of wandering, he wears a large, wide-brimmed hat that hangs low on his head, obscuring much of his face. Lean and tall, his frame is bent and twisted under the weight of his burden – an old burlap bag, tattered and slung carelessly over his hunched back. Its contents rattle as he strides down the road, a ragged and gaunt shadow, a horrific Saint Nicolas, gifting nightmares and darkness to all he visits.

Occasionally pausing to observe certain homes, he cranes his neck from side to side, and then turns and continues on his way. In rare instances, unsatisfied by what he gleans from the scrutiny of his observation, he pauses a moment longer and drops his bag to the ground. Rashly emptying its contents before him in a clamorous instant, bones and teeth of all sizes clatter out, scattering across the stone. Then, as quickly as he's strewn them out, he frantically begins to gather them up again, tempestuously counting and examining each item before placing it back in the bag, ensuring that everything is as it should be. If no one from the house he stands in front of hears him before the completion of his frenzied inventory, there will be a death in the home before the year ends.

The *abuelas* say that long ago, in a time before even they were young, he was the handsome son of a wealthy family. His parents spoiled him, giving into the young man's every wish without hesitation. One morning when he woke, he asked his father for a meal of his favorite meat – venison. His father happily complied, trudging out into the wilds to find a deer. But there were no deer to be found that day, and he returned empty-handed. The mollycoddled boy flew into a fury, and no matter how much his father tried to console him, his anger only grew. In the blinding rage of his tantrum, he thrust a large hunting knife deep into his father's chest. Crimson streaks flashed from the wound, but soon subsided to a gentle flow of sticky warm red, pooling on the floor, soaking into the boy's clothes as he knelt over his father's corpse. His hands drenched in treacly, gooey blood, he stabbed the knife's blade over and over into the dead man's chest. Clumsily slicing and hacking, he found his father's liver, removed it, dressed it and took it

to his mother to cook for dinner. Soaked in cream and sautéed with onions, she served the boy his meal, then went to take a plate to her husband, only to find his butchered body. Her screams brought her father-in-law to her side, and between her sobs and howling cries, she told him how his son had come to be in such a state, as well as what had become of his organs.

Tearing the boy from the table, his grandfather dragged him out of the house by the scruff of his neck and threw him to the ground. Stripped naked and tied to a post, the old man lashed the child until his own hands were bloodied and blistered, and the boy's bones were starting to become visible.

The old man then gathered his own son's hacked-up remains into a large bag, and tied them around the boy's neck. He kicked the child into the street and set two hungry dogs upon him, condemning him to carry his father's bones with him until the end of time.

The old grandfather could not have known the unfathomable evil he released into the world the day he cursed this little boy – who is now known as El Silbón.

It is said that when he is not stalking villages and towns, he roams the countryside, hungry for death and accustomed to the taste of men. He prays on those whose absence will be neither noticed nor mourned – abusive and womanizing men, drunkards and thieves, and those who find advantage in the darkness of night. Sucking the liquor out through his victim's navel, he then tears them limb from limb, as easily as he would a roasted chicken. He feasts on their flesh, saving their organs for last. When finished, he tosses their fleshless bones into the bag with his father's.

Don't make the mistake of believing that your wholesomeness will spare you this gruesome demise. While El Silbón prefers the flesh of the wicked, his hunger knows no difference, and his malevolence knows no bounds.

PUTTING YOUR PURSE ON THE FLOOR WELCOMES MISFORTUNE

LOST MONEY · LOST JOB · LOST PROSPERITY

BEST TO KEEP YOUR PURSE NEARBY AND AWAY FROM THE GROUND

A NOCTURNAL CROW IS AN UNWELCOME OMEN

BEWARE

THE ROOSTER'S CROW

◄— PAST DARK! —►

VILLIANY IS ABOUT AS SOMETHING UNNATURAL IS ON THE PROWL

NEVER PASS THE SALT DIRECTLY INTO ANOTHER'S HAND

FOR FEAR OF KICKING OFF A ROW

PLACE IT ON THE TABLE AND ALLOW THEM TO PICK IT UP THEMSELVES

ALWAYS SETTLE YOUR FEUDS BEFORE MAKING DINNER

NEVER MAKE TAMALES WHEN YOU'RE ANGRY

MASA WILL NOT FLUFF UNDER

THE VEXED HANDS OF A FURIOUS COOK

AN ANGRY CHEF MAKES

● SAD TAMALES ●

UNFLUFFED · DRY · THICK · HEAVY

⌁ THE GREEN LADY ⌁
HAWAII * UNITED STATES

The gulch dips starkly down, cut from the landscape of orchid and coarse vine clinging to kauri trees, rainbow eucalyptus and pili trees to a damp, low-growth bed of soil and detritus that is blanketed in the deep greens of tree ferns, wild ginger and loulu palms, and dotted with the bright reds and yellows of the heliconia that thrive in its brackish groundwater. The beauty of this gorge deceptively shrouds its unforgiving nature and subtly masks its cataclysmic potential. Running all the way from nearly the top of the volcano Haleakalā to the ocean, even the slightest rain can transform this gulley into a river. But when a Kona wind comes, a violent and unpredictable storm brings heavy rains that rush down the side of the volcano and through the gulch, washing anything in the gulley out to sea. They say it was the torrent from a storm like this that took her child from her all those years ago.

She preferred crossing through the valley than taking the bridge. It wasn't so much that the traffic was bad on the bridge, but more that she had an unwarranted fear of these new horseless carriages. So, just as a gentle rain began down in the lowlands, she descended the soft soil walls of the gulch, holding tightly to her young son's hand as she traversed the damp ground. High up, however, shrouded in dense cloud, a heavy rain was falling on the peaks of Haleakalā. The stream she walked beside had become a raging torrent 4,000 feet higher up, and without any warning, a deluge of water crashed down upon them and, in an instant, her son was gone.

As she clung to the hard rock on the wall of the gulch, she screamed her boy's name into the rush of water, fearful that he was gone, yet hopeful that perhaps he too had found a foothold. When the storm finally passed, the boy's fate was unfortunately apparent.

First, she asked the villagers for help, and for a time some of them came to her aid, helping her to scour the beaches and lower wetlands for any sign of the child. However, when nothing was found, their numbers dwindled and in less than a week it was down to her alone, walking the gulch looking for her son. The villagers watched on, knowing her search was senseless, and over time, as their kind words started to become insincere encouragements, and their concern turned to apathy, they eventually stopped noticing her at all. Nonetheless, she was always there searching – the love of a mother is unfathomable. For days, weeks, months and years,

LEAVE TO HAWAII WHAT IS HAWAIIAN

TAKE NOTHING NATURAL FROM THE ISLAND AWAY WITH YOU!
NOT SAND FROM THE BEACH NOR ROCK FROM THE VOLCANO
NOT EVEN THE PLANTS FROM THE GROUND

PELE

GODDESS OF FIRE WILL CURSE YOU AND MISFORTUNE WILL FOLLOW YOU ON YOUR WAY

NEVER SLEEP WITH YOUR HEAD NEAR A WINDOW

THIS IS HOW A DEMON FINDS YOU
AND TAKES YOUR HEAD AS ITS REWARD

NOR SLEEP WITH YOUR FEET NEAR A DOOR

THE NIGHT MARCHERS MAY DRAG YOU OUT INTO THE NIGHT
TO JOIN THEM IN THEIR ETERNAL CAMPAIGN

BEWARE THE SPIRITS OF CHILDREN WHO WILL JUMP IN AND HITCH A RIDE
KEEP YOUR CAR WINDOWS CLOSED NEAR A GRAVEYARD
THEY MAY EVEN FOLLOW YOU HOME OFF THE ISLAND

NEVER HARM A BLACK MOTH

DEFINITELY DO NOT KILL IT AS IT MAY BE THE SPIRIT OF A
LOST RELATIVE PAYING YOU A VISIT

this woman returned again and again to the gulch looking for her missing child. As time passed, she became more and more wild – more a part of the untamed gulley than civilization, and in the end, she finally disappeared into the deep viridescence of the jungle.

Decades passed, and although her name has been lost to the mists of time, her story has not. Consumed by the pain and longing for her lost boy, the torment of her exhausted soul somehow sustained her. Over time, as less and less of her remained human, her will and desperation drove her to become something else.

The clothing she once wore is now long decayed, ravaged by the moisture of the jungle. Her skin, once soft, has become viscid green, and sprouted with verdurous young orchids and ginger intertwined with vine. Her hands are now made of strong knotted and twisted roots, and her fingers are coarse, gnarled tendrils. Her teeth, too, have gone, replaced now by jagged, mucky splinters. Seaweed hair clings damply over her head, and down her shoulders and back. The smell of dead fish and vegetal decay lingers in her presence, and a dank, unpleasantly claggy air surrounds her. What was once her devotion to a tender reunion with her lost son in time has become an obsession to reacquire that which she perceives has been taken from her.

Nature cruelly stole her only child, and now the Green Lady has become the personification of that cruelty. Any child she comes across, she steals – snatching them up and taking them for her own – never to be seen again.

···❀❀ CAMAZOTZ ❀❀···
HONDURAS

A dankness hangs heavy in the air as you near a small black void in the rock ahead. The slight opening, barely noticeable, seems not only to be swallowing what scant illumination remains from the day, but also to be effusing a viscous darkness into the night. You edge so gingerly into the abyss, until at last, a great cavern opens up, enveloping you in silence.

In the immense emptiness of this vast cavern, torchlight casts a narrow cone through the blackness and dissipates into the void. As strange as the silence is, as your hearing acclimates to its stillness, an even stranger sound starts. Faint at first, but in time more obvious, you hear the soft rhythmic lilt of breathing. Torchlight wildly whirls around you, left then right, then behind, finally streaking upward to the stone ceiling. High up above, stalactites hang, packed tightly, seemingly huddled together in a wholly unusual formation. As your torch pans across the strange construction, one of them appears to move – just a mesmerizing wriggle at first, and then an unfolding, like some great leathery origami being undone, revealing a head crowned with horns and coarse black fur, a short, upturned nose above a yawning sharp-toothed mouth, and two small, blinking black eyes.

The entire ceiling appears to come alive, unfolding and stretching as if awakened from some ancient slumber, and hundreds of black eyes now gleam through the darkness. These are the descendants of a god – a powerful and unforgiving king, ruler of the underworld – the lord of sacrifice, death and the night. What he lacks of the divine, this, his horde, make up for in numbers. Clambering across the ceiling, clinging to hard stone with their black nails, they hook and claw, heads whirling and swiveling. High-pitched chirping and sharp, staccato clicks echo through the open cavern, lending sight to the sightless. Terror drives you toward the opening in the cave wall, but large, leathery wings unfold in the darkness as one of these massive batlike creature dives and snatches at the air around you. With less care than when you entered, you quickly make your way out into the night air.

Your heart pounding, you scuttle down the rock wall with the sound of flapping wings beating heavily against the air, swirling overhead. Even here, under the open night sky, your safety is uncertain, and you stand in the uneasiness of the dark shadows, all the while knowing that the darkness belongs to them.

···❦❦ LA DIABLESSE ❦❦···
TOBAGO

The full moon hangs low in the sky. Cool night air drifts across the island as the warmth of the setting sun still rises from the dusty ground. There is frog song and the sound of crickets in the distance as she strolls along lonely Paria Morne Bleu Road humming a soothing melody, wordlessly casting a bewitching spell.

Occasionally a fellow traveler passes by, tips his hat and offers a "*bòn nuit*." She nods in return, the large brim of her hat dipping and rising as she gives a slight pull of her voluminously layered skirts in a demure curtsey. As usual, the passerby takes an increasing interest in her and tries to engage her in conversation. With a tilt of her head and a curtsey less shy, in sultry tones she asks him for a favor: "Would you be so kind as to accompany me to my home?" She offers him her gloved hand, knowing that once he takes it, he is hers.

Infatuated by her beauty, the man believes that if he agrees to her request, he will have her, so they walk on. "Just a bit farther," she says, as they walk the winding mountain road. Seduced by her ambrosial scent and soothing tone, his thoughts fixate on his eventual lustful conquest. As he ponders the slimness of her figure, he is oblivious to the distance they've walked. Unaware that they've left the road and have begun to walk along mountain paths, he ponders only upon the delights concealed beneath her gown. Deeper and deeper into the jungle they walk, as his licentious intentions continue to mount.

Now standing on a high ledge, they look out over the vista as she removes her gloves. The layers of her skirt lift slightly in the mountain breeze, and reveal a cloven hoof hidden beneath her gown. His passion recedes as horror washes over him, yet he still cannot overcome his lustful desire. Inexplicably, he takes her hand – ice cold and rigid. She turns to look at him, her face now shriveled and transformed into a wicked skull-toothed grimace. As she cackles maniacally, she makes her final request, "Give me a kiss."

His corpse is found the next day at the bottom of a ravine, broken and shattered, with a look of unimaginable horror on his dead face. The authorities declare it a suicide, but can't help but wonder why he would jump off the ledge backwards.

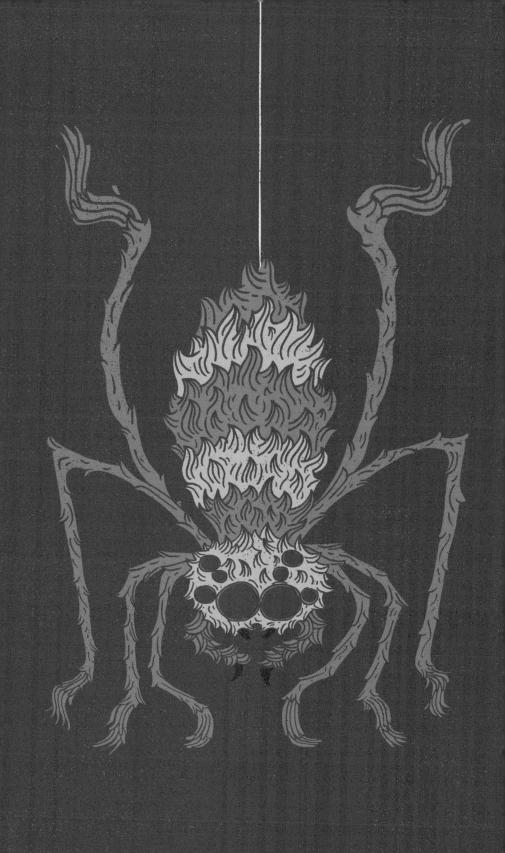

CARIBBEAN LORE

NEVER SPEAK NEGATIVELY ABOUT SOMETHING THAT HASN'T OCCURRED YET

IT MIGHT COME TRUE

DON'T HAVE A GOAT MOUTH

NEVER WISH EVIL UPON ANOTHER PERSON

IT MIGHT COME BACK TO YOU

YOU MAY WANT TO CHECK ON YOUR WIFE WHEN YOU SNEEZE

BE AWARE OF A BUNNER MAN!

MISSING A LOOP WHILE PUTTING ON A BELT MEANS YOUR WIFE MIGHT HAVE A MAN ON THE SIDE

PUT A HOT PEPPER IN FOOD THAT TRAVELS AT NIGHT

WARD OFF EVIL SPIRITS

ENTER YOUR HOME BACKWARDS AT NIGHT
SPIRITS WILL SEE YOUR FACE AND NOT FOLLOW

BEWARE

THE TWITCHING OF AN EYE

SOMEONE IS SPREADING GOSSIP ABOUT YOU AT THAT VERY MOMENT

BROWN GRASSHOPPER

IN YOUR HOME MEANS MONEY IS COMING YOUR WAY

GREEN GRASSHOPPER

IN YOUR HOME MEANS MONEY IS ABOUT TO FLY AWAY

···≈⊰ DOUEN ⊱≈···
TRINIDAD

The forest closes in as darkness falls, deep shadows stretch and yawn as if waking from their daylight slumber. Almost a whisper, easily dismissed as a slight breeze, the cries of a young child break the nocturnal stillness, "Mah-mah ... mah-mah." Again it cries, this time closer, and every bit as heart wrenching.

From the shade of the undergrowth, small and naked, a cherub-like being appears. Two tiny glowing eyes peer out from beneath a large straw hat, this face a manifestation of an unbaptized soul, featureless and blank save those piercing eyes and a small, lipless mouth. With a tiny hand outstretched, again in whimpering tones it pleads, "Mah-maaaah ... mah-MAH." Just then another appears, and then another, all begging insistently, "Mah-maaaaaah . . . mah-MAH," for the warm embrace and lost love of a mother. It is an emotional plea aimed directly at the sympathetic nature of a parent, and one moment of your concern is all that's needed for these creatures to snatch your own child. The ruse is up as the darkness erupts with laughter. Wild with terror, you search for your child – he has vanished alongside those little beings who only moments ago had your heart. You hear your child through the darkness, his voice muddled with the giggles of the Douen. You call his name, pleading, only to hear it echoed back in mocking voices and sneering cackles. Soon, the sun will rise and daylight will illuminate what seems unfathomable – your child is gone.

You'll search the forest and find occasional tokens of hope – a scrap of fabric or a button from his pajamas. You'll find footprints, following them through thickets and rivers, brambles and marshes, but infuriatingly and inexplicably, they always lead you back home.

Small reminders will appear from time to time: a collection of shells from your child's favorite beach; a bowl of his favorite berries left on the stoop. Each gift leads to a desperate hunt, only for you to find yourself once again standing in your own yard. Days pass and you remain trapped in this nightmare.

One night, you wake with a start, finally remembering a detail that until this moment has escaped you – through the weeks of endless searching, frantic panic, haunted by the loss of your child. Pursuing the fiends who stole him, tracing their tracks over and over from start to end – but it's their feet you finally remember. Their feet were facing backwards.

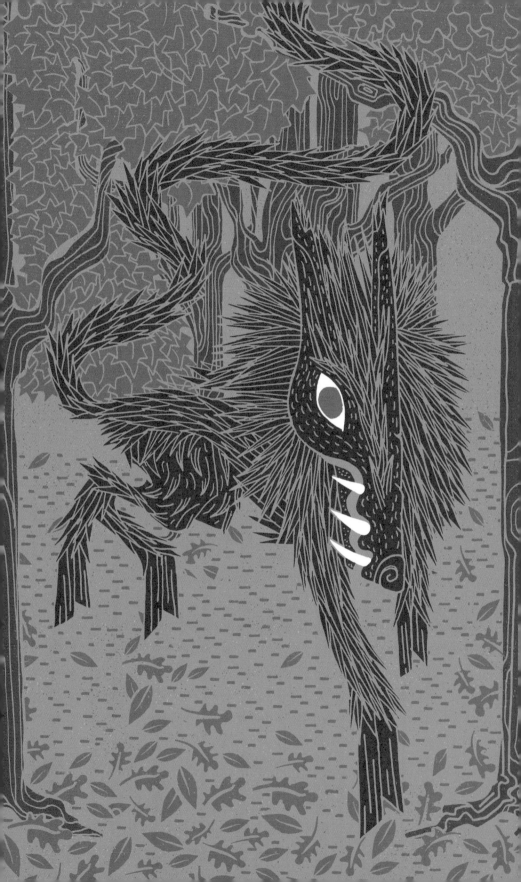

❦ EL CADEJO NEGRO ❦
CHIAPAS ✳ MEXICO

The night is dark, the heavy clouds hiding even the brightest of stars. Along the forest path, desperate shadows seem to reach out from the obscurity, choking all light. In the far distance, two red embers glow. There is an emptiness in this darkness – an emptiness that somehow feels like it is less than nothingness.

The two burning coals come closer. The scent of filthy animal – of a goat that has been left tied up for too long, unkept and untended – lingers in the humid air. The sounds of the jungle fall away as an eerie stillness presses in. The beast nears, eyes aflame, its very shape radiating darkness and shadow. Its fur is knotted, black and twisted, a mass of wiry coarseness. Its nostrils flare as it breathes deeply; the creature can seemingly taste the scent of you from afar. A heavy chain flatly clanks with each nod of its head.

Torrents of fear wash over you, and though every fiber of your being screams "Run!", now is not the time to flee – that moment has passed. The beast makes its languorous approach, each stride punctuated with the sound of a heavy hoof crushing rock and twig against the gravelly path.

And now the gaping maw of the Cadejo Nero is upon you, its teeth rotting within its broad jaws. Hot brimstone breath tousles your hair and burns your lungs. Coarse, sharp goat-hair scratches your skin while the beast slowly circles you. Immobilized with fear, you do not utter a sound; although trembling, your feet remain soundly planted on firm ground. To speak now would mean a lifetime of fearful insanity, to run would mean a sure and violent death. Through deep sniffs and heavy sighs, every inch of you is inspected; your life is laid bare before him, and all your doings and misdeeds are scrutinized. You close your eyes and await your judgment.

Crickets sing, a light breeze brushes your cheek and you open your eyes. The darkness has lifted, and along with the heaviness in the air, the Cadejo Negro has gone. Your life judged and found worthy, you continue onward, down the path.

A SONG SUNG DURING THE EVENING MEAL WILL ATTRACT EVIL SPIRITS

LUST · GREED · DESIRE · CONCEIT

EVIL

 AN UNMADE BED

IS AN INVITATION TO THE DEVIL TO CLIMB IN

EARLY MESOAMERICANS BELIEVED THAT REFLECTIVE SURFACES
COULD BE USED AS PORTALS TO A WORLD WHERE SPIRITS DWELLED

MIND YOUR MIRRORS

TWO MIRRORS PLACED ONE FACING THE OTHER CREATES A PORTAL
FOR DARK SPIRITS AND NEFARIOUS ENTITIES TO ENTER YOUR HOME

DARKNESS CONCEALS THE MOST VILLIANOUS DEEDS

FILLING THE SHADOWS WITH THINGS UNSEEN · SWALLOWING THE DAY IN INKY NIGHT
IT HAS NO WEIGHT NOR MASS NOR FORM TO GRASP · SOUNDLESS AND CALM IT SURROUNDS US STILL

COLD IRON

CARRY A PIECE OF COLD IRON AS PROTECTION AGAINST THE MALICIOUS MEDDLING OF THE SUPERNATURAL

KEEPS THE SPIRITS AT BAY • DISCOURAGE THE DESCENT OF FAE FOLK

BURY AN IRON KNIFE UNDER YOUR DOORSTEP TO PREVENT UNINVITED WITCHES FROM ENTERING

BENEVOLENCE • MERCY • KINDNESS

GOOD

THE NUMBER SEVEN

SEVEN HEAVENS GRACE THE SKY • SEVEN SEAS SURROUND THE LAND

SEVEN CHAMPIONS MARCHED UPON THEBES AND THE SEVEN SAGES BUILT OUR SOCIETY

SEVEN DAUGHTERS OF ATLAS LIVE IN THE NIGHT SKY AS THE PLEIADES

HANG A HORSESHOE

THE DEVIL CANNOT ENTER ANY PLACE WHERE A HORSESHOE HANGS OVER THE DOOR

THE ENDURING PURITY OF LIGHT

A BEACON IN THE NIGHT • THE LIGHT AT THE END OF A TUNNEL • THE BREAK OF DAWN

THE LIGHT OF BUT A SINGLE CANDLE BRINGS COMFORT IN THE DARKNESS

THE SECURITY WITHIN THE CITY WALLS

NEVER LOSE SIGHT OF A TALLEST STEEPLE • NOR THE SOUND OF ITS RINGING BELL

► BEWARE THE WILDERNESS ◄

KEEP TO THE SAFETY OF KNOWN FOOTPATHS • MIND THE DARKNESS OR ITS SHADOWS

⸙ EL CADEJO BLANCO ⸙
CHIAPAS * MEXICO

The stars gleam brilliantly in the summer night, basking in the amber light of a low full moon. Shadows dance as streaks of moonlight filter through the jungle canopy, and the path is lit up with the brilliance of your lantern. Up ahead of you, two blue flames gleam luminously against the cobalt sky, casting a blue aura upon everything. These illuminations seem to have a life of their own, a living and welcoming brilliance.

The scent of sweet, freshly cut hay drifts along on the gentle breeze. The jungle has fallen quiet, and a feeling of sacredness permeates the stillness. A creature draws near, its flaming blue eyes brightly burning amid a blanket of soft white fur; its coat shines in the glow of its eyes' dazzling blue gaze. The animal is fettered by a large chain which clanks dully with each slow nod of its head as it sniffs the air. Waves of warmth crash over you as you eagerly await this beautiful creature's approach. It lopes toward you, each of its strides punctuated by the sound of a hoof pushing lightly off the gravelly path.

Now upon you, the Cadejo Blanco bows its heavy head before you, pressing its luscious soft fur into your hand as if requesting your affection. It slowly circles, giving you the opportunity to stroke its entire coat. With its head low, its muzzle explores the scent of you, its warm breath comforting and fragrant. You stand silent in your joy, caressing the magnificent beast with long strokes through soft white hair, enveloped in the exuberance of this beautiful animal. Through its deep sniffs and heavy sighs, you feel as if your life has been laid bare, and the Cadejo Blanco is bringing you more joy than you could have ever imagined. You close your eyes and drink in the moment, awaiting your judgment.

A soft growl cuts through the silence as a pointed muzzle nudges your eyes open. Sharp white teeth lay bared below a crinkled and snarling maw. With its back hunched and its hackles raised, the Cadejo Blanco paces around in front of you. Your life, judged and found lacking, will end now, right here on this path.

► HERE HAVE BEEN TOLD BUT A FEW OF THE HORRORS OF ◄

NORTH AMERICA!

► **YET BE WARNED** ◄

OF THE MULTITUDE OF TALES UNTOLD

AN UNKNOWN HORDE OF GRUESOMENESS
OCCUPYING THE VAST EMPTINESS AND
EXPANSIVE WILDS OF UNTAMED LAND

DENSE WOODLANDS AND UNINHABITABLE DESERTS AND DEEP LAKES
RAGING RIVERS AND HAUNTED STREETS AND ABANDONED TOWNS

► STILL MOST OF ALL ◄

BEWARE

THE DARKNESS THAT RESIDES IN THE SHADOWS OF WHAT IS KNOWN

· TREAD LIGHTLY · STAY TO THE PATH ·
· MIND YOUR SURROUNDINGS ·

~~❦❧~~ INDEX ~~❦❧~~

·✦ ACKNOWLEDGEMENTS ✦·

You wouldn't be holding this wonderfully frightening book in your hands without the passionate storytelling enthusiasts at Watkins Media Limited. I owe an immense amount of gratitude to my publisher Fiona Robertson, who first asked for something truly terrifying from North America. A collection of folk tales and illustrations, "but not for kids". A request that instantly became our beacon, our true north, the lodestar of the book. Thanks also to Karen Smith for the beautifully designed pages, for the color, typography and layout as well as a handful or two of wonderful ideas that made this book what it is. To Kate Crossland-Page, who ensured only the best words were used and transformed my sometimes-rambling storytelling ways into an anthology of beautifully written stories. Daniel Culver, who kept the whole project moving and on time. Steve Williamson, who meticulously found every misspelled word, incomplete thought and incongruity of image and tale. The publicity and marketing team, Laura Whitaker-Jones and Hayley Moss, for making sure the book gets seen. The sales team, Lauren, Monica and Yuliia, who allowed the book to find its way into your hands, and the folks in rights, Melody, Lisa and Olha. Thanks to the entire Watkins team, who have truly made this book come to life.

Many thanks also to V. Castro for the amazing foreword and thoughtful comments on the importance of folk horror in telling our own and our communities' histories. I'm also thankful to have grown up in the state of Wisconsin, honestly one of the strangest states in the Union. From my childhood in the Driftless Area and the years in the Northlands, I'm thankful for the strangeness of Wisconsin. To the city of Eau Claire, where I began to find my purpose. To Christos Theo, an amazing professor, advisor and friend who helped me find a direction when I needed it most. My friend and mentor Juelie Sires, who provided the encouragement and the environment to first put my skills to use. And to the friends who pushed and inspired me to be both a better person and artist: you are often in my thoughts whenever I lay pen or pencil to paper. And, finally, to my wife Natalie: thank you for all the support, endlessly listening to stories and fielding requests for opinions on topics as varied as what shape of head is most frightening to which shade of red best represents a pool of blood at midnight.

✦·—··—·✦

~⚜ ABOUT THE AUTHOR ⚜~
* MIKE BASS *

I have always loved a frightening story, although the reasons why have evolved over time. When I was young, they were a distraction. They provided a name for the things in my real life that terrified me. You see, I grew up in a house with spirits. Not the ones of contemporary cinema, rotting flesh, razor-sharp nails and constant torment; no, my spirits simply never stopped making you feel their presence. An oppressive pressing, a dark weight and indescribable sadness. Sure, there were the occasional outbursts, items thrown across the room, knocks and bangs, a shaking bed in the middle of the night and even disembodied voices, but for the most part, they simply made  sure their existence was known. For young me, naming the monster under the bed gave me a means to prepare for the moment it might strike.

As I got older and moved on to university, the days were brighter. I was away from the heaviness of home and at the same time, I found art. Yet, with every move, every new apartment, I waited for the first sign that I wasn't alone. As I found some homes to be quieter and others a bit louder, story returned. This time in my own voice, and along with my own illustrations. I sought out old tales of hauntings, listened to people's first-hand accounts, and scoured the reference section of the library. I guess in a way I was looking for tales that helped explain the experiences of my own past. In the process, I found a joy not only in folk horror, but in folklore itself.

Starting with the folklore-rich tales of Wisconsin, I've spent years pairing illustrations with the tales they derive from. I've sold my prints at art fairs as well  as in the bricks-and-mortar shop Zip-Dang, in Madison, Wisconsin, which I own with my wife Natalie. I'm the author and illustrator of the *Folklore Oracle* card deck, in which I explore the many ways folktales connect us not only to other cultures but to the civilizations that came before us. You can find more of my artwork and writing on my website InkandStory.com as well as on Instagram, Facebook and Threads @wiscomythos.